Praise for A SNICKER OF MAGIC

An ALA Notable Children's Book
A *New York Times Book Review* Editors' Choice
A *Parents Magazine* Best Children's Book of 2014
A SIBA Okra Pick

★ "This tale offers all [the] earmarks of fine storytelling, including colorful, eccentric characters, an original, highly likable narrator and a mighty 'spindiddly' plot." —*Kirkus Reviews,* starred review

★ "A delightful and inspiring debut." —*School Library Journal,* starred review

★ "From every angle, Lloyd's first novel sparkles and radiates warmth . . . Working in the folksy vein of Ingrid Law's *Savvy,* Lloyd offers a reassuring, homespun story about self-expression and the magic that resides in one's mind and heart." —*Publishers Weekly,* starred review

"The story [touches] on helping others, budding friendships, and strength of family. First-time novelist Lloyd has produced a 'spindiddly' product that will hearten word and poetry lovers and encourage those who have almost lost hope for a happy ending." —*Booklist*

"Its intricate plots and subplots about a magical town hooked our kid reviewers and, through a character who collected words 'serendipitously,' taught them vocabulary. The kids described it as 'spindiddly'—the story's made-up word for better than awesome!" —*Parents Magazine*

"Lloyd's novel has much more than a snicker of magic. It offers a vast and varied cast of characters, a multilayered plot, and a bit of mystery along with the fantasy. But the best of all is Lloyd's ability to make this story feel so real that it could be taking place next door." —*Christian Science Monitor*

"Lloyd's story takes many unexpected twists and turns [and] should be read aloud for maximum enjoyment, with a pen handy to jot down new words, preferably not on your sneakers. Young spelling enthusiasts, Scrabble lovers, Boggle big leaguers and word people of the world—hang on for the ride! Felicity Pickle will take you places, and that, fellow logophiles, is spindiddly, indeed." —*New York Times Book Review*

OVER the MOON

NATALIE LLOYD

Scholastic Inc.

Copyright © 2019 by Natalie Lloyd

This book was originally published in hardcover by
Scholastic Press in 2019.

All rights reserved. Published by Scholastic Inc., *Publishers since
1920*. SCHOLASTIC and associated logos are trademarks and/or
registered trademarks of Scholastic Inc.

The publisher does not have any control over and does not
assume any responsibility for author or third-party websites
or their content.

No part of this publication may be reproduced, stored in a retrieval
system, or transmitted in any form or by any means, electronic,
mechanical, photocopying, recording, or otherwise, without written
permission of the publisher. For information regarding permission,
write to Scholastic Inc., Attention: Permissions Department,
557 Broadway, New York, NY 10012.

This book is a work of fiction. Names, characters, places,
and incidents are either the product of the author's imagination
or are used fictitiously, and any resemblance to actual persons,
living or dead, business establishments, events, or locales is
entirely coincidental.

ISBN 978-1-338-11851-3

10 9 8 7 6 5 4 3 2 1   21 22 23 24 25

Printed in the U.S.A.   40
This edition first printing 2021

Book design by Nina Goffi

For Justin—for everything.
I would fly anywhere with you.

Once there was a girl brave enough
to draw a question mark in the
dust that covered her heart.

1

Mallie Ramble

Dustflights are trained to sense explosions in the Down Below.

Honeysuckle is my papa's Dustflight, a tiny yellow bird they give every miner in Coal Top. When I was a little girl, Honeysuckle brought me heaps of comfort as I watched Papa walk to the mines. I couldn't go with him to the Down Below. But our brave yellow bird could. She perched like a speck of plump sunshine on his shoulder

She'd coo lullabies in his ear if he got lonely. She could keep him safe. Papa hasn't been Down Below in more than a year now, but Honeysuckle stays right near him most of the time. Until the work whistle blows. That's when she floats down to Windy Valley to find me.

Alloo, alloo, Honeysuckle sings against the window. I run to the glass and raise it just a notch. A cool, dusty breeze carries her sweet birdsong into the room. The sound is a hint of home, and for a second, I forget I've been covered in dirt for hours. Honeysuckle snuggles her feathery face against the pane.

"I'm hurrying," I promise her. And she sings a chirpy tune to help me speed up cleaning Mrs. Tumbrel's floors.

That's one of the reasons all the miners get a Dustflight when they start work in the Down Below; their sweet presence helps you work faster. Here's another: The birds can warn the miners if they've gone too deep. Or if they're about to find gold. Not that anybody finds much gold these days. Mostly, I believe the birds are a tactic the Guardians use to get kids to join up young. In a town the color of dust, who wouldn't want a bright yellow bird they can take home every day?

I stretch my stiff neck and hear a cluster of pops. The fingers on my left hand are clenched in the cold rags, so I stretch them straight, slowly. One by one. My hand will stay that way, eventually. Bent and clawed like I'm always clutching rags. *Old maid's grip*, mountain people call it.

Honeysuckle taps the glass lightly with her beak, her way of telling me it's time to get out of my slop pile and get on up the mountain. My mountain. If I miss the train, I'll have to walk to the top. I did that once, and I will never do it again. For as long as I've been alive and breathing, I've heard stories about monsters who roam the woods at night. I used to think our parents made it all up just so we'd stay close to home. Now I know better. Still, sometimes I wonder if walking through the monster woods is any worse than being around valley people. They can be monstrous, too; these snooty folks who want their floors cleaned and toilets scrubbed and powder cakes made just so, *just soooo*.

I stand, balance the bucket full of filthy water in the crook of my right arm, and haul it back to the kitchen, careful not to slosh it over the newly polished wood. My right arm ends just below my elbow, but I've never had a problem getting things done one-handed. I'm not going to lie: Sometimes I think it'd be nice to have two grippy hands. Especially when it comes to opening stuck windows. Braiding hair faster. Carrying this nasty muck bucket around. Scrubbing floors might go by a little quicker, maybe. But it doesn't matter much. I was born this way, so I'm used to it. And besides, I'm a fast worker.

I check my Popsnap to make sure it's secure—that's my fake arm, complete with a fake hand, that I keep attached to my right elbow when I'm working in the valley. *This way you'll blend right in*, the valley doctor told me. *It's a universal color that fits everybody.* Thing is, Popsnaps only come in pale orange. I've met all kinds of people, who look all kinds of different ways, but I've never met a soul who's orange.

I spin around quickly when the front door squeals open. This is payday, and there's nothing that makes me prouder than giving my family the money I've earned for all of us: Papa, Mama, and my little brother, Denver. We need this more than ever today.

We *have* to have this today. Money's not just running low for us Rambles. Our money has flat run out.

The front door slams shut, and four kids—wild as mountain chickens—run screaming across the floor I just mopped.

I lurch forward and nearly yell—QUIT IT!!—but the words gob up inside me. *Be gentle*, Mama always tells me. *Be gentle in the valley.* That's her polite way of telling me not to get so fired up down here. Not to argue. Not to disobey. And I get it: I'm all the income my family has now. I have to keep this job. So I clutch my apron, bite my tongue, and watch the ruckus. The Tumbrel kids stomp red-clay clusters and clots of grass all over my handiwork. Their mother—Mrs. Tumbrel—saunters through behind them, bracelets jangling. She clutches her velvet skirt and lifts it, trying to avoid her offspring's sloshy path of yuck.

She snarls at the mess on the floor. Then she looks at my right elbow, at my Popsnap.

"I worry you aren't capable of the work, Mallie," she says with a sigh of fake concern. "Finding another mountain girl might be best for us both. Perhaps you'd be better suited for other chores."

"No! I'm perfectly capable." I try to sound calm and submissive. Gentle, like Mama says. But I'm not a gentle soul. I'm still learning many things about myself, but I already know this much: I'm wild and brave on the inside, a fire-popper in a glass jar. Some days I can't help but spark a little. Some days, my heart is a raging fire.

"Don't misunderstand me, sweetie. You are . . . an inspiration!"

I bite my tongue so hard I wonder if it might fall off. Mrs. Tumbrel knows only two things about me: my name, Mallie Ramble, and that I have a Popsnap where part of my right arm should be. Neither one of those things makes me inspirational. She's only saying this because my arm looks different from hers. That is called pity. And pity feels like an insult. Words leap off my tongue before I can cage them: "If your children hadn't—"

"Hadn't what?" One black-inked eyebrow arches at me.

I gulp, trapping the words I really want to speak back down in my heart. "They must not have realized I'd just finished these floors. They tracked mud all over the place!"

"Mmm." She cocks her head at me, thinking. Does she really not believe I'm capable of scrubbing a stupid floor?

She saunters close enough to peer down her long, regal nose at me. "I'll keep you on, Mallie. Because I am a good woman. But some advice: Having high spirits will make it hard for you to find another employer. And you already have your loss working against you." She glances at my right arm again and clears her throat.

She's always looking at my Popsnap. Just flat-out staring at it. I get having a little bit of curiosity about people—I'm a curious soul myself!—but she can't even make eye contact with me. Sometimes I imagine pulling it off and throwing it at her so she can have a good long look and be done with it.

"Here, now. For your work." She drops two Feathersworth in my hand.

That's only two days' wages. She hasn't paid me in a week.

"Mrs. Tumbrel, I don't mean to be disrespectful. But this is the wrong amount. I earned—"

"*I* decide what you earn. Remember that before you unleash your temper again. And anyway, these are hard times." Mrs. Tumbrel flutters her eyelashes dramatically. They look like little ink bats, flapping over her lying eyes. Because I *see* the velvet bags of goods she brings in every day. The new dresses she wears. It's not that the Tumbrels don't have enough money. They just don't feel like paying me.

But the words *Yes, ma'am* float out of my mouth. And the coins make a dull jangling sound when I drop them in my apron pocket.

"Finish this before you leave," she says dismissively, waving at the floors as she walks away.

No time to grumble, so I lean in to the day:

Bucket, refilled.

Knees, grounded.

Lean in, Mallie, lean in.

Finish strong,

Finish proud!

I don't see the shiny brown boots of my enemy until they're right in front of me, tracking more sloshy lines of mud and crud across the floor.

2

Open Windows

"Better hurry, Coal Top." Mrs. Tumbrel's oldest son, Honor, stares down at me. If I didn't know Honor so well, I'd believe what girls in class used to say about him: that he's storybook beautiful, with pale hair, tan skin, and pretty eyes. But I *do* know him. And I've picked enough apples from the orchards in Coal Top to know that what looks shiny on the outside can be rotten at the core. This is why looks don't mean a Feathersworth to me. Looks tell you nothing about a person's soul.

He smirks and rests his hand on the spiraled handle of the shiny sword strapped around his waist. It's a gift from his parents. In case he ever has to fight the monsters, they said. Ha! It's all I can do not to laugh out loud just thinking about this scenario. Honor Tumbrel would only use one thing if he got close to a monster: his running shoes. Still, he's been showing off that sword for weeks. He probably holds it when he sleeps.

"You don't want to walk through those monster woods alone, do you?" he continues, leaning down closer. "They might eat you." He glances at my Popsnap. "What's left of you, at least."

I pull my rag from the bucket and wring it out on his shoes.

"What the—"

"My mistake," I say sweetly.

He glares at me, eyes shining with menace. "Remember what we used to call you in school? Before you had to quit? We called you the mountain pirate. Maybe you should get a hook next time instead of a Popsnap."

I fight not to hide my arm from Honor's mean gaze. I'm not ashamed of my body—not any part of it. But that doesn't change the hurt when he teases me. It takes effort to fold my arms in my lap, casually, and pretend his words didn't settle inside me.

I look him square in the face. "I do remember. That's what you called me at the May Day Races last year, when you were beside me at the starting line. Just before I out-ran you."

Slowly, he crouches down until we're closer—too close—eye-to-eye. Just as he's about to speak . . . a shiny blue piece of paper slips from his pocket, swooping down to the floor, where dark water stains spread from the corners.

Are you still brave enough to dream?
WANTED
Brave and wiry young fellers*

Honor snatches it away before I can read the rest.

"That's not for your eyes, mountain girl." He grins as he shoves it in his jacket pocket. "It's for somebody going places. Not for a girl covered in slop water."

I close my eyes against the inevitable: Honor kicks the dirty bucket so it sloshes all over my dress, and all over the floor.

"Take my clothes home and wash them." He drops a stinky bag of his laundry in my lap and walks away, smiling. Honor's rotten mom buys him new clothes every week. But he still gives me his dirty laundry to take home and mend. "See you tomorrow, Mallie in the Muck."

Angry tears—tired tears—warble in my eyes as I refill the bucket. Again. And lean back in to work.

I want to scream. So, I decide to sing instead.

Well . . . first I look around to make sure nobody's within earshot. Singing's not allowed in the valley or on the mountain. Not unless you're a bird. Even the Guardians can't control wild things—like Dustflights.

Like me.

Singing could be deadly up on the mountain, they say—we'll take in too much Dust. But I'm not on the mountain right now. I keep my voice soft and low:

Mountain girl, lift up your eyes,
the stars are shining bright for thee.
Reach out and take the silver cord.
Braid beauty now for all to see.

Honeysuckle chirps madly at me from the window, flapping her wings against the glass. Her wing tips make little dot prints all along the Dusty pane. At first, I think she wants to zoom inside and peck Honor's eyes out, and I wish she would. But then I realize she's trying to get my attention. I suck in a quick breath when I realize why.

Something nearly invisible, the size of a feather, floats in through the open window.

It's flat as a ripped piece of paper, crisscrossed with hundreds of tiny veins of color.

Just the sight of it makes me catch my breath.

A Starpatch.

They're so rare these days that I think my tired eyes must be playing tricks on me. Starpatches are leftover beauty from a better time, a time way before I came along.

Here's the story I know:

Years ago, before the Dust came and covered the skies, mountain people took starlight and wove it into cloth: clothes and blankets and spangled capes. Those dreaming clothes settled over weary shoulders, giving them adventure and hope—and peace—as they slept. And the dreams settled over the sleepless and reminded them tomorrow would be better, even if today broke their hearts. The ability to weave starlight would be magic enough—all by itself. But there was a better magic than that, even.

The better-than-best magic, we called it.

But we never talk about *that* anymore.

Some memories, even sweet ones, are too painful to discuss.

The ending is always the same anyway: The Dust swept over us and snuffed out the stars.

People claim they've seen patches of light here and there, floating on a forgotten breeze. *Maybe there's light left over*, they say. *Maybe sometimes the light finds a way through.*

I reach up—gently—and take the bright patch between my muddy fingers. Flatten it against my palm.

This is how starlight feels:

> cool like wind,
>
> soft as a feather,
>
> special as a spoken wish.

My little brother will love to see this, I decide. He'll be as happy as I am to know there's a little piece of bright magic still floating through this dark world.

The Starpatch pulses so bright against my hand that I feel like it's alive somehow. A solid thought settles immediately in my heart. As sure as I know my name, I also know this much is true:

I am still brave enough to dream.

3

Familiar Faces

The light dims low in the valley, spreading shadows all around town as I run for the train station. There's not much light around here to start with. The Dust has covered the sky—blocking the sun and the stars—for as long as I've been alive. That's twelve years. But the Dust stretches back several years before that. We only know the sun is setting when dim gets dimmer, then so dark that the world looks swallowed whole.

As I scramble through the muddy streets of Windy Valley, the firelight lamps flicker awake. I pull the scarf around my neck up over my nose, and see folks I pass do the same. Clouds of Dust settle thick in the valley when the night presses in. That Dust weighs you down, if you breathe in too much of it.

But it doesn't do any good complaining. That's what Mama told me when I first groaned about working for the Tumbrels here in the valley. And then she taught me this trick: When the present situation is abysmal, you go some-place else in your heart. So, I rethink it this way: I might *look* like Mallie in the Muck. But in my heart, I'm Mallie over the Moon. Flying to worlds unseen on wings made of Starpatches. I bust up the Dust. I smash it. I bring back the light. The light . . . and the better-than-best things that went away with it.

Allo, allo. Honeysuckle pecks my cheek, soft as a kiss, and grabs my attention before I run through a mud puddle.

"Good eye, Honeysuckle!" I tell her, and we make our way through the busy streets toward the train stop.

Mountain girl, lift up your eyes,
the stars are shining bright for thee.

I hum the old mountain tune as I pass a row of stores. The Starpatch flickers like butterfly wings in my pocket.

Star-goods used to sparkle brightly from the shop windows here. The brightest things in the valley now are the roofs on the Guardians' houses. Those are the men chosen to take care of us. Pointy golden spires are affixed to the corners of their copper-plated rooftops, like rusted crowns scattered all over the valley.

The house with the tallest spires belongs to Mr. Mortimer Good. He's the Head Guardian of the mountain and the valley. I've never seen the man. Most people haven't. But we've heard all about him. Mortimer has slain more monsters than any Guardian in history. Little kids pretend to be him, using sticks for swords when they battle in the streets. I pretend to be him, too, sometimes.

The train hasn't arrived yet, so I duck around the corner of the building and slink down against the ground for some rest. This is my favorite hiding place. I can see everything happening on the platform.

Close my tired eyes.

Cough when the wind blows a sheet of thick Dust past my face.

Two. Feathersworth.

Their weight in my hand is nearly nothing. Almost as light as the weight of the starlight in my pocket. The money won't last us a week.

Tears burn the backs of my eyes, but I refuse to let them fall. It'll send Mama into a frenzy if I walk in a crying mess. She has enough to worry about.

Smudge-faced kids from the valley mines are showing up on the platforms now, all sleepy-eyed with yellow birds perched on their shoulders. They're waiting for the train that takes us all an hour's ride back to the top. I stay hidden but strain my neck, hoping to see a face I've dearly missed.

And there he is. The sound of Adam Peyton's voice is an arrow; it shoots through the crowd all sharp and sweet and hits me square in the heart. I bounce up on my tiptoes to get a better look at him. He's standing tallest in the center of a group of boys. Hat cocked sideways on his head, just like he used to wear it. Scarf looped around half of his face, too—green and frayed, too thin to be much of a barrier to the Dust. A small, happy heat radiates in my chest. That's the same ratty old scarf I made him for winter holiday two years ago.

Adam has been my friend for as long as I can remember. But we haven't spoken in almost a year. *That's common*, Mama tells me. *Some friends—even the most wonderful—are only meant to be in your life for a season.*

But I don't care for that way of thinking. Mostly because I thought my story would always be tangled up with my best friend's story. Now I miss him so bad my heart aches.

The boys are dressed in drab coveralls and covered in coal dust. This is probably why the flicker of blue in their midst catches my eye. Adam's holding a blue flyer like the one Honor Tumbrel had. All the boys are looking at it. Whispering over it. They look so fired up about the thing, my brain's practically burned up with curiosity.

I should say something.

I should call out Adam's name.

So what if it's been a year?

We're still best friends . . . aren't we?

The scream of the train startles me, drowning out the voices of the boys on the platform. A small, familiar face looks frantically from one of the windows. That face is looking for me, and it's my favorite face in the whole world. Denver.

As the night, and the cold, presses in around us, the train circles slowly toward the town on the tip of Forgotten Mountain: Coal Top. I always imagine this train looking like a big steel snake.

Hissing as it climbs.

Bright eyes beaming into the darkness.

And we're all here stuck in the belly of the beast . . .

The night wind howls as it blows against the steel. A lantern swings from the ceiling at the front of our train car, sending firelight flickers across our faces with every jolt. I glance down at my little brother, Denver, and pull him closer against me. Mama let him ride the train down to pick me up. That was a fine idea. His face made me feel even happier than a Starpatch. As soon as I saw Denver's face, I forgot about everything that hurt.

Denver's hair is curly, soft as dandelion fluff. *Wishing clocks* is what my mama calls dandelions. That is a fitting way to think of my brother, too—so small and magical to me. A wish come true. From the first time I saw him, I knew I'd never love any person more than I loved Denver Ramble. He's seven now. Nearly eight. Denver is still at the Coal Top school, which is the reason I'm not. Once Papa got hurt, one of us had to go work. They've sent young children into the mines before, even small, scrawny seven-year-olds like Denver. But that won't happen to him; I'll make sure of it. The thought of Denver crawling around for hours in darkness makes me ache, bone-deep.

He's chirped about the view all the way up the mountain, his voice softening as Honeysuckle settles in his lap for a nap. "I could see six mountains through the Dust on the way down!" he says.

"Do you remember their names?" I ask.

Denver draws peaks in the Dust on the window as he recites the familiar rhyme:

There's Mount Carson,
Pink but defiant,
The mighty Pembers,
Our snowy giants!
The Lightning Range will sizzle and slay,
Only the truly brave will stay.
The Bogs are so squishy,
Mirror Mountain so bright,
That old river Timor will give you a fright . . .

He pauses, chewing his lip. "That's all I can remember."

"That's a lot!" I tell him. "And those are the closest anyway. Well done. Do you remember how the rhyme ends? All tipped in gold, they call for thee . . ."

"Such beauty for the brave to see." Denver's chest is puffed in pride as he finishes my sentence. I loved learning mountain lore when I was his age, too. I used to love the view from the train. I'd imagine being a brave explorer. Climbing every unknown peak. Discovering whatever lies past it. But nobody leaves Coal Top or Windy Valley—sudden and violent clouds of Dust can rustle up anywhere, anytime. Plus, the climbs are too treacherous. The way is too dark. To say nothing of the monsters that roam at night. Here, the Guardians keep us safe.

"I'm glad Mama let you come down to ride with me," I tell him, comforted by the warm weight of him against me. "Promise me you'll never get off the train to look for me if I don't make it to the platform. You ride back up. Okay?"

"You promise, too." His voice is small and steady in the darkness. "Don't walk alone in the night ever again. I don't want the monsters to hurt you."

A shiver rolls over my shoulders, and I can't help but glance outside. The darkness is ashy pitch, pressing up against the windows. Are shadows moving out there—or is it just the lights of the train making it seem that way? The dark and the Dust are so thick together that I can't see into the woods surrounding us. I don't know exactly what's out there watching us. Stalking us. But I know it got close to me once. And I know I never want that to happen again.

"Mallie." Denver says my name as gently as a hug. "Tell me about what it was like before the monsters came."

I nod. Stories are a fine way to pass time. I begin the sweetest tale I know:

"Many years ago, the mountain people weren't afraid to walk at night. Night was their favorite time, in fact.

24

There were no monsters in the woods back then. There was no Dust in the air.

"Forgotten Mountain was a very different place. It had a different name, for starters—Bright Mountain. And what made it so bright wasn't the sun, even though it shined gold and glittering back then. It was bright because the stars loved us, and we loved them back. Mountain people could weave dreams from starlight."

"Tell me how they did it," he whispers. "Tell me the better-than-best thing."

I speak low, in a reverent whisper: "They say that each night, the Weavers would wait on the mountain peak. Wait . . . until a warm gust of wind announced the arrival of the Starbirds. They were horses, huge and wild, with shining manes and wings that shimmered in the night. They would land on the mountain, and then the Weavers—young and old, anybody brave enough—would climb on their backs and sail into the sky."

Denver smiles a crooked-tooth grin.

"The Weavers went soaring, collecting those long beams of starlight, those patches of stardust, gathering and weaving and sometimes volleying the light back and forth to one another. Mama says that we were the kings and queens of the mountain.

"The horses loved the mountain people. Children, especially. They used to come and play with them in the woods. Carry them through the forest."

Denver Ramble keeps a near-constant shadow of a smile on his face. The dimple in his cheek is always there, ready to deepen. The tilt of his mouth is always up, aimed for a grin. But his smile fades to a flat line when he finishes the story that we all know too well: "And then the Dust swept over us. The stars were snuffed out. And those beautiful creatures flew away . . . I hope they flew somewhere good."

For a time, we sit in silence, rocking in rhythm as the train churns upward. Mourning a memory we never got to experience. It's not just the wonder of it all that I wish we still had.

Without the starry coats to wear, dreaming's not as easy as it used to be. We all have nightmares now. The Dust can weigh you down if you let it. Our hearts are more fearful than peaceful.

"I believe they'll come back someday," Denver says suddenly. His voice is chirpy and sweet, like always. But his chin is high. His jaw is set. "They'll come back. They'll find a way through the Dust."

The Starpatch in my pocket flickers wildly.

4

Dustblobs

With a scream of the whistle, our train emerges from deep woods onto the platform of the train station in Coal Top. Men from the mines are gathered around small fires, drinking stale water from copper mugs. Jabbering with one another about the day's events. Some are hunched over near the fires sleeping, too tired to even make it all the way home.

"Watch it, Mallie!" Denver says, grabbing my arm and pulling me to the side as I step off the train. He points to an oozing, tar-colored blob as it splatters the ground. A Dustblob.

Starpatches used to settle in the treetops here. Now the Dust gets so thick it sometimes sticks to the dew in the trees instead. Gobs up and warbles on the branches, like inky cocoons about to burst. Dustblobs can't hurt a person, not physically. But having one of those things splatter on your shoulder will break your heart for days. You're left with a particular kind of sorrow you can't shake. The time one landed on me, I felt like I was breathing in sadness for weeks.

"Thanks," I say. Denver takes my hand, and it's a perfect fit, a key inside a trusted lock. *I'll protect you*, I think. *I'll never let anyone hurt you*. We walk together down the platform. The cool night wind swirls patterns through fallen leaves. Out of the corner of my eye, I see Adam help a girl off the train and walk the same path with her. I feel a funny zing somewhere inside my chest.

The only shops we have left in Coal Top are closed for the day. Our stores aren't fancy like the ones in Windy Valley. Ours are ramshackle huts huddled against the tracks. They used to be a sight to behold: star-goods sparkled so bright people had to squint to see them properly.

Star-goods didn't last long, Mama told me once. But that was fine: The stars weren't greedy—they always shared their light. The Weavers bent that light into tangible things people could hold and keep. Some could pay for star-goods. Some couldn't, and that was okay. We had plenty back then for everyone.

Now there are only the mines' company stores: places to buy new shoes, hard hats, lanterns, coveralls, and—of course—baby Dustflights.

"Mallie." Granny Mab calls me over to the platform, where she's setting up her cart. Maybelle Fry is nobody's real grandmother, but everyone on the mountain calls her Granny. Actually, some people call her Granny *Mad* instead of *Mab*. They think she's an eccentric old saleslady. But I think she's a fine artist. Granny Mab pushes her rickety old cart through town selling all manner of trinkets. Broken lanterns, books and dolls, mirror rocks and faded quilts.

Tonight, she looks like a little witch setting up her display. Granny Mab wears a black dress that hits just above her knees, along with black-and-white-striped socks. A black top hat crowns her wavy white hair. The hat's so folks will remember her, she says. As if anything about her is forgettable.

She lets Denver sift through her wares as she speaks softly to me. "You need to hurry home tonight and keep your brother close to you. Tell yer mama that the crows are on the mountain."

"The crows? I don't understand."

Granny Mab shakes her head. "She'll know what I mean. Hurry home and tell her, all righty?"

"Granny Mab! Is that you?" A man staggering down the platform calls out to her in a hoarse, frantic shout. He's straining to support a man much bigger than him. A crowd of folks gather around them as they move closer. "It was a Dustblob that got him! Dripped down from a tree before I could catch it."

Granny Mab reaches—gently—and lifts the injured man's bowed head so she can look into his eyes. That's when I see the tar-colored blob of ooze dripping from his right shoulder down over the center of his chest. Over his heart.

Granny Mab moves fast. She grabs a brown bottle from her cart and squints at the liquid swirling inside. She shakes it up, pops the cap off with her teeth, and pours the contents into a chipped teacup.

"Mallie," she says sharply, pulling my attention from the men on the walkway. "Fetch the blue jar on the other side of the cart."

I'm moving before she finishes telling me, and when the jar is in her hand, she adds its contents to the cup, too. A tiny swirl of purple smoke *poufs* from the cup, then vanishes.

"Clean him up," Granny Mab instructs. The man's friend takes his handkerchief and wipes up what he can of the Dustblob. The stain remains.

"Have him sip slowly," Granny Mab continues, her voice a gentle crackle. "Easy breaths between sips. Tell him you'll sit with him till the sorrow passes."

Most everyone has stopped to see the commotion—adults and children alike. I'm touched by the way the man's friends step close, rest their hands on his shoulders and arms. "I'm here, Will," they say softly. A stray dog snuggles his face into Will's open palm.

"Mallie!"

I startle and look up. It's Mama yelling for me. She's walking toward me, lantern lifted high. Worry's thick in her voice. Why? She knows that Denver's safe with me. I'm perfectly capable of walking him home myself.

Granny Mab reaches Mama before I do, passes along the message I was supposed to give. Mama squares her shoulders and reaches for my brother. "Come. A storm is blowing in, I think. Let's get home."

When Mama and Papa were young and newly in love, they built us this home in the North Woods of Coal Top. They only wanted a small place, just a perch hidden away from the world. Even as the sky grew dark, even as the

Dust covered Windy Valley and the towns all the way up the mountain . . . they could still see the stars. They were the last to lose their light.

Now the skies are only Dust. The tall trees are full of Dustblobs. And the only light we have comes from the fire always crackling in the hearth. But I think there's a light that comes from the way we love each other, too. I know I feel warm as soon as I'm with my family.

Papa is settled in a chair near the fireplace when we walk in, lantern light bright across his face.

"Hey, Papa Bear," I say, resting my small hand on top of his large, freckly one. His long fingers wrap around mine, holding on tight. Papa's freckles are the reason I'm extra proud of the spray of freckles across my nose. Even when Honor Tumbrel made fun of them at school. I remember my papa taking my face in his hands and saying, "But, Mallie . . . a face without freckles is like a sky without stars!"

Oh, how I miss that voice.

His voice was the first thing to go—lost somewhere in the Down Below. My uncle said it happens pretty often to the men. He saw the voice fly right out of my papa's mouth, like a wild bird turned loose from a cage. With Papa's voice gone, the rooms are empty of their songs and stories and of the three best words in the world:

I and *love* and *you*.

That's what I miss most—not just the words themselves, but the way Papa said them. The mines took those words from me. They've taken other things, too. Papa lost his sight to an explosion. The Guardians in the mines said it was his own fault, that he was too careless with the machinery. But I know that's a lie. My father is a man who cares about everything.

Papa's accident put us in a predicament: He doesn't speak. And he does not see.

So, he can't work in the mines, and his pay's withheld because the explosion was "his fault."

Women have never been allowed Down Below, so Mama can't go.

Boys grow up and go into the mine.

Girls make the city sparkle and shine.

It's a stupid rule, but we've said it as long as I can remember. And anyway, Mama takes care of Papa. So that leaves Denver. And Denver is not an option, which leaves me.

Snap-hiss, the fire pops.

Alloooo, Honeysuckle whistles softly.

Mama locks the door and glares out into the darkening woods. Dark, and strangely quiet.

Papa lifts his face toward the sound of the bolt locking.

"Crows on the mountain," Mama mumbles softly. Papa's

strong, tattooed arms reach for Denver, who climbs on his lap. They hold each other like they're bracing for a storm.

And that's when Honeysuckle lets loose: She sings out a shrill cry of alarm that makes every hair on my arm feel like a prickly pin.

There are no avalanches here above.

There are no explosions on land.

But there are bad people.

BOOM

    BOOM

    BOOM

—the sound of steel-toed boots kicking the door.

My voice comes out rusty: "Who is it, Mama? What do they want?"

Papa's already up, shoving my brother toward me. Mama rushes at us.

"Hide him," she says as she shoves us both toward the ladder to the loft beds. Honeysuckle's singing so loud I can't hear anything else Mama says. Denver stumbles toward the loft ladder. I latch my good arm around him. Boost him up as high as I can.

"OPEN UP," booms a man's voice from outside. "Cain Ramble—open this door!"

I scramble behind my brother, my boot slipping on the ladder rungs. I've climbed to the loft all my life with one arm, but I've never had to do it this fast before. It's harder than I thought it'd be. Near the top, I fling myself into the loft, latch onto Denver, and we pull up the ladder. We scramble underneath the bed. The front door bangs open. Denver trembles in my arms as we hear heavy footfalls fill the room downstairs.

I try to control my breath as I stare through the slats in the floor and see three tall men, all dressed in black. Their boots make every floorboard tremble. Plumes of Dust rise up as they move.

The Guardians are here.

Their black capes ripple as they walk into the room, and I remember Granny Mab's words: *The crows are on the mountain.*

"You have no right to barge in here like this," Mama yells. Honeysuckle's still singing her angry tune. And I can't see Papa's face from here, but I know it's filled with fury, too. His voice might be gone but he communicates fine with his eyes. If those men are brave enough to look him in the eye, they'll cower. I don't care how tough they act, or how rich they are.

"Get out of my house!" Mama yells again.

The man in front ignores her. The Guardians always do this; they don't think women are worth listening to. "Cain Ramble?"

"I speak for him now," Mama says. "He lost his voice in the Down Below. You know that. What business could you possibly have with my husband at this hour?"

"Not with him," says the voice. "With your boy."

5

Crows on the Mountain

With my left arm, I clutch my brother hard against my chest. He doesn't cry. He doesn't whimper. He presses his head into the nook of my neck. We're both sweaty with fear, trying not to breathe too hard, too loudly.

Oh, but I want to breathe hard; I want to breathe fire at those terrible men. Part of me wants to dare them to try to take him. I don't look strong, I know. But sometimes I can feel a wild strength rising up inside me.

"Denver's not here," Mama says. Her voice doesn't waver. She's rehearsed this lie. "He's with family in the valley. Won't be home till spring."

"That so?" the Guardian asks, and I hear him moving around. "You'll be in prison by then, Mrs. Ramble. In prison for massive debt."

A nearly silent gasp lets loose from Denver's chest. *Shhh*, I beg him. *Shh.*

"We've got a month's worth of wages left," Mama says. "And our girl is working, too. It'll be just enough to get by, and that's all we need."

"That's not how we see it," says the Guardian.

And he begins to list our debts: the medical expenses, our housing cost, the machinery my papa "broke" Down Below.

I'm so angry I'm digging my fingernails into the wood floor, wishing it was the bad man's face.

"You'll pay your debt like everybody else, Mrs. Ramble. Your boy can use some of his wages, if he works hard enough. If he doesn't, we'll take your house, your clothes, everything you own. The longer you wait, the worse it's going to get."

"This is outrageous!" Mama yells. Papa shakes his head at her—*no. Don't make them madder.* But I'm proud of her for finally yelling. Being gentle has gotten us nowhere.

"You send the boys too deep," Mama shouts again. "You expect too much. Men and boys are losing their voices down there. Losing their sight. They're dying down there."

The man shoves Mama to the floor. Papa lunges at him, and I flinch when I hear the Guardian's fist meet with Papa's belly. I pull Denver close and *Shh, shh*, I beg him. *Don't make a sound.* Tears stream down my face. Down Denver's face.

The Guardian's voice is so calm when he speaks. "Turn over four thousand Feathersworth in one week, or your boy will report to the mines."

"Four thousand Feathersworth?" Mama says, with a mirthless laugh. "We can't find that kind of money in two years, let alone one week."

"Then we'll take what we're owed in other ways."

The door slams.

Silence fills the room.

Silence . . . and then the sound of Mama and Papa on the floor.

Crawling toward one another.

Sobbing softly.

The Starpatch I caught earlier pulses, forgotten on the floor beside me.

6

The Invitation

The next morning, I'm awake before any other Ramble. Even Mama. I gave my heart some space to break last night, but now it's morning. It's a different day. And I don't have time to despair. I have to find a way to save my brother.

Braiding my hair takes time, even when I'm not in a frenzy. But I move fast:

dress over my head,

boots on my feet,

my Popsnap attached.

I run out the door on tiptoes so I don't wake anybody else. The air in the North Woods is frigid and biting, stinging my face as I close the door behind me. Honeysuckle flies out just before I hear the click.

"Don't worry," I tell the bird, my breath floating into the cold air as we run through the woods. "I'll fix this. I can fix anything. I'll ask Mrs. Tumbrel for more work. Some families hire girls to live with them, you know. To take care of them all day and all night—I'll ask if I can do that." The thought of this—plus my lack of breakfast—makes my stomach churn. "Or . . . maybe she knows someone who might need me? Who could pay me more?"

Doubtful. Mrs. Tumbrel barely thinks you're capable of working for her. It's not Honeysuckle telling me this, of course. It's the logical side of my brain. But it's true.

At the platform, Ms. Marcia Bloom is setting up her morning pastry stand. Apple puffs, tiny round pies dusted with cinnamon, are the most popular food here on Coal Top. I don't have money to spare for an apple puff, but the warm smell of them baking makes my stomach growl as loud as any monster on the mountain.

The thought slams against me: Denver will be so hungry in the mines.

I run through a zillion scenarios of how I can come up with four thousand shiny Feathersworth—fast—while Honeysuckle bobs along beside me.

Maybe I could work for two families.

Maybe I could sell stuff—like Granny Mab. Learn to bake special cakes—like Ms. Marcia. It's a shame I can't work in the mines instead of Denver. The conditions are miserable, but the pay's dependable at least.

I'm tempted to close my eyes here and pretend I'm Mallie over the Moon again. Soaring up and away from my worries. Flying back to a time before the Dust. But there's no time for daydreaming now. Today I have to plant my boots right here in this place and fix things.

I love the stories about the mountain, the time before the Dust settled in: the creatures who lived here, the kindness we shared, the starlight in the trees. I wish we still had all of that. But I would settle for a world that didn't punish a man for getting hurt or being unable to work. It makes me want to punch something. Punch a hole in the Dust so we could have the stars back.

The Dust. I've wandered into a small cloud of it that

people have kicked up along the train platform. It's scratchy in my throat when I breathe it in. But I don't cover my nose or mouth; I keep on pacing. The longer I pace, the angrier I get.

Honeysuckle chirps loudly—like an alarm in my ear. I startle and step out of the Dust.

My temper simmers.

Be gentle, Mallie . . . I can hear Mama say. And another wave of nausea overwhelms me. I've never wanted to actually hurt anyone. I don't want to do it now, either. I'm just tired of being gentle. I growl in frustration and kick a rock onto the tracks. I mope to the side of the building—the side where I hide every day to catch my breath. I slink down to the ground and look up. Boards are crisscrossed above me, holding clusters of paper flowers that were put there— I'm guessing—to make up for the fact that nothing much grows here anymore. Above the dusty petals, I see grayish brown sky, tinged with swirls of dull yellow. Like a dandelion smashed in mud. It's as close as we get to sunrise. Angry tears drip down my face in a solid stream. Honeysuckle gently taps my cheek where the teardrops settle.

"Tickets for the early riders, please!" the station-master yells. "Train's approaching!"

My breath catches. I shove my hand in my dress pockets, even though I know it'll come up empty. In all the frenzy yesterday, I didn't lay out my ticket this morning. I reach into Honor Tumbrel's laundry to see if he left one in his pants pocket. But my fingers trace over something else. Something shiny, blue.

The flyer . . . the one all the boys are talking about. Honor must have picked up an extra one.

I unfold the stupid, mysterious piece of paper he didn't want me to see. I read over it, quickly this time:

Are you still brave enough to dream?
WANTED
Brave and wiry young fellers*
unafraid to ride and race and fly in the fear of
certain death!
Do you long for adventure? For riches untold?
For a home in the valley?
Come closer, then, brave dreamer!
<u>**Great riches await!**</u>
Interested parties meet in the West Woods
on the first morning of autumn,
by this invitation only.

*Orphans preferred.

None of this makes sense, of course. But my heart jolts over two words:

Riches untold.

That sounds very nice. Forget the fact that I'm not a feller. Or an orphan.

Maybe sometimes all the praying and pacing and hoping convinces the universe to cut you some slack. Because this flyer in my hand—this strange invitation—it feels like a gift. Like an option that could actually work.

This is the first day of autumn. This is the change I've needed, maybe the change that could make everything right. A new idea blooms out of my brain:

"It's a few hours till the second train comes," I whisper in a rush, just loud enough for Honeysuckle to hear. "Here's the plan—I'll go to the woods, see what all this hubbub is about. If it's nothing, then I'll catch the late train and talk to Mrs. Tumbrel. Easy!"

Honeysuckle does not look convinced that this plan will be easy. She's all fluffed up and quiet, glaring at me with her beady brown eyes.

"Maybe not easy," I admit. "But doable!"

As far as I can see, the only thing stopping me has to do with the fact that I'm not a boy.

"That's the easiest problem I've solved this morning," I tell Honeysuckle.

I dump Honor Tumbrel's stupid laundry out on the

ground, grab a pair of slacks and a shirt, and run into the woods to change.

Pants buttoned (that takes forever). Shirt tucked. Velvet blue jacket notched in place. Then I flip my head over and stuff my braid up into his hat. (This, for the record, is when it would be kind of nice to have two grippy hands.)

I keep the shirtsleeves long so my Popsnap might be less noticeable. Whatever this task is, I don't want the organizer to think I'm incapable. Or, worse, an inspiration.

With fire in my bones and a mission on my mind, I wave to Honeysuckle: "Let's move!"

And I'm off for the West Woods!

"Mallie?" I go still. That's Adam's voice. And it's coming from behind me.

I already heard the second whistle from the mines. That means all men and boys are belowground now, beginning their daily descent. Once the second whistle blows, it's too late to show up. You don't get paid for the day.

I turn around slowly. Adam is standing very still, watching me. Holding his own blue flyer.

"You missed your whistle," I say, pretending everything else is normal. Including the fact that I'm wearing Honor Tumbrel's clothes.

Adam looks shocked to see me. His eyes are wide, forehead scrunched up like he's got a zillion questions. Or like he's just flat confused. "What are you doing here?"

"I am going into the West Woods for riches untold," I say, holding up the flyer and stomping to where he stands. "And I am going to win them." I have to stand on my toes to be eye level with Adam now. When did he get so much taller than me? How could he look so different in such a short amount of time? His features are sharper now, too. And his eyes . . . I gasp.

He smiles sadly at me. "You've seen eye stains before, Freckles. Don't act so surprised."

"But you've only been down there a year . . ."

Eventually, all miners' eyes turn coal black, so dark you can't see an iris separate from its halo of color. Just like Adam's. Dark ink is already creeping over pale brown, blotting out the sparkle I used to see there. I think about what Mama said about boys in the mines: how it grows them up too fast. It's a sad thing that boys in Coal Top crawl underground in the prime of their life, when they should be left alone to grow in the sun.

He looks away from me, down at the blue flyer scrunched in my hand. "Where'd you get that?"

"Irrelevant."

He groans. "Please get on the train. Whatever that flyer's referring to . . . it definitely isn't safe."

"I don't need safe! I need riches untold."

"I have a feeling that this"—he holds up his own blue flyer—"it's going to be truly, terribly dangerous. Plus, you're about to miss a day's work, Mallie. That's a full Feathersworth!"

"I'm averaging two Feathersworth a week due to my sunny disposition and my terrible employers," I tell him. "Riches untold sound better."

"Mallie . . ."

"Adam. They came for him last night. For Denver . . . We hid him upstairs. They didn't take him but they'll come back. They'll search the house. I'm out of ideas. I'm out of options."

Adam's face softens as I tell him the story.

"That's a lot of Feathersworth," he says.

"More than I make in years."

"Maybe I can help." He says this in a strong but thoughtful way. And I know he's already thinking of ideas. "If this works out, I can bring you some money . . ."

"No," I say. "We both have families to take care of. I can do this, too." I hold up the flyer. "I'm doing it. So, there's no sense in trying to stop me from going!"

"You're not a feller," he says with triumph, jabbing his finger at a line on the page.

"You're not an orphan!" I yell at him.

"All aboard!" the conductor yells from the platform.

Adam steadies his voice as he responds. "They *prefer* orphans. You know what that means, right? It's dangerous enough they don't want us to leave any family behind."

The thought sends chills across my heart. "I'm brave enough."

"I never doubted that," he says. His mouth quirks into a half grin. Just like it used to. But I can't get past the change. Inky black eclipsing the hopeful brown. "Okay," he says, resigned. He knows I don't turn back once I fix my mind on something. "We'll go together."

As if he is the one giving me permission!

"Yes, we will," I say, folding the flyer into the pocket of Honor's pants. "I'll lead the way."

We walk in silence through the dusty forest, hesitating when we finally get to the border of the West Woods. I'm waiting for Adam to tell me to turn back again. But he doesn't say a word.

Long, thin brambles curl out over the boundary line— their thorns sparkling even without any sunlight. The Dust seems to billow extra thick above us. Herding us, it feels like. Pushing us into these sinister trees. Dustblobs warble in the treetops and gnarled-limbed shadows stretch out across the forest floor.

A sound from somewhere deep in the woods makes me jump backward. A rasping scream. It didn't come from a person. It sounded animal-like. Predatory. I've heard that scream before. I hoped I would never ever hear it again.

I heard it the time I walked through the woods alone, home from my first night of work in the valley. At first, I thought the footfalls were human. But I was wrong. I was being stalked. If I moved faster, it moved faster, until I was running from something—from a scream—so close to me I could feel the warmth of its breath.

It made the same sound. *Exactly* the same sound.

"Men in the mines say there are more monsters in the woods every day now," Adam says. "Especially the West Woods." His jaw is clenched, but I see a tremble in his hands. I'm trembling, too. "Are you afraid?"

"It's possible," I confirm. "But I'm going to pretend like I'm not. I'm going to pretend I'm Mallie over the Moon."

He raises an eyebrow and smiles. "Who?"

"Never mind. I'm just glad we're together."

He nods. "Me, too."

Side by side, we keep walking.

Dustblobs dangle like dead leaves in the treetops of the West Woods. It's hard to see in here; the tree canopy is thick and the shadows stretch long and wide. These woods are darker than mine. But they're still just dusty woods, I remind myself. Adam and I are familiar with the forest. So why does this batch of trees feel different? For a time, we talk just to hear the sound of our voices. Just so we can both pretend we aren't afraid.

"I didn't mean to be so rude back there," he says as we step over tangled roots and fallen leaves. "I don't want to be that way with anybody. I just didn't want you to get hurt. I always pictured you getting a scholarship eventually. Heading off to school in the valley. Doing something amazing."

"You know that won't happen for me."

"Anything good can happen, Freckles." He's quiet again. Our boots slosh through a ditch thick with mud. We're mostly walking side by side, occasionally reaching out to help each other. Just like we used to.

"Careful," he says, guiding me around a pile of dull, yellow dirt. "That's Timor powder."

"I've never heard of it."

"They use it down in the mines for medicine. To heal cuts and stuff. It works fine, I guess. But too much of it makes you feel weird."

"Are the mines pretty terrible?"

"Yeah," he says as we walk. "I always knew I would hate it down there. I had to go, though. Dad can't work Down Below anymore. He made it longer than most men do. I mean, I'm nearly thirteen and I've only been in the mines a year. That's something to be grateful for."

"That's true. They like little kids, if they can get 'em."

He nods somberly. "We won't let them take Denver, Mallie."

We don't speak for a time, and this is fine with me. Silence feels as good as conversation when you're with a true friend. I think about all the times we'd walk quietly together—miles of sweet silence—then one of us would bust out in a run. Just for the feel of it. But running or walking, we were always together. Pace for pace, exactly the way best friends should be. I wonder if he misses those days as much as I do.

"Watch your step," he says, extending his hand so I can scoot past a briar bush. "We came here together when we were kids once. Remember? But we never made it past the boundary line."

I smile. "Yes—a bird flew at us, swooped down and scared us half to death."

"Scared you," he clarifies.

"You ran just as fast and hard as I did!"

"I'm not running this time." His voice has a sad kind of resignation to it. "I'm just flying into the face of certain death."

"Good thing I'm here to save you if you need me."

"Don't flatter yourself, Freckles." He grins, and my heart warms.

He grips my arm, suddenly.

"Listen," he says, nodding his head in the direction to the side.

There's someone else in the woods.

7

Brave and Wiry Young Fellers

More people. Lots of people. Footsteps come from all directions, breaking bony tree limbs on the forest floor. Snapping sounds echo all around us.

Adam turns me loose and whispers: "You can still go back."

"Shut up."

Boys suddenly emerge from the woods around us. It's like they just appeared out of the shadows. Some of them are taller than Adam, older, with big muscles and smug grins on their faces. They stomp through the woods with ease. Some are as small as Denver. One little boy even has the same hair color as my brother. He's tiny, dressed in slacks, a T-shirt, and blue suspenders. Round glasses perch sideways on his face. I know the look on that kid's face— when you're trying to look brave, but you're scared out of your mind.

"Ooof," I gasp as I slam into the ground. A cloud of Dust rises around me.

One of the boys just shoved me out of his way as he walked past. "Pardon me, mountain trash," he chuckles. I look up to see him pushing other people out of his way, too. My insides turn cold at the sound of his voice—and the sight of the sword on his hip. I would know that rotten voice anywhere. Honor Tumbrel. I know he won't recognize his own clothes; he has so many that he couldn't care less. But I definitely can't let him see my face.

A feeling between anger and sheer adrenaline launches me off the ground. I can be rough, too, I decide. I slap away Adam's outstretched hand, shoving my way past Honor and all the other boys twice my size. I follow the crowd to a large clearing in the West Woods, pushing my way to the front. There are only around thirty of us so far, but it wouldn't matter to me if there were a hundred. I'm earning those riches untold today. And I need to be at the front of the crowd to figure out how.

Two Guardians herd us to the center of the clearing. They don't look at our faces or our flyers. "Move along!" they yell. *Easy enough*, I think. *I'm in!*

I glance around frantically at the woods, trying to see through them, past them, to whatever it is I'm supposed to be fearful of. Why *did* they ask for orphans?

I swallow down my fear. I pray nobody sees my knees knocking together.

Present situation: My legs are here in the West Woods.

But in my head—and my heart—I'm home with Mama, Papa, and Denver. We're safe and happy and no man—no Guardian—will ever hurt us or take us away from one another.

A small wooden stage has been built in the center of the clearing, with steps leading up to it. We all flock toward that stage in a slow, steady push. A couple of Guardians stand at the corners, more around the perimeter of the clearing—all with swords at their hips. They're stoic, faces gaunt and wiped clear of expression.

Are they here to protect us?

Or to keep us from running away?

I hear Adam call to some of his friends: "Wilder! Connor! Nico! Over here."

Thanks a lot, Adam, I think. I know all those guys from school. I pull my hat low over my eyes so they don't recognize me and blow my cover.

"Why's Honor Tumbrel here?" Wilder says. "I thought it was just boys in the mines?"

Connor shakes his head. "Every boy got one—on the mountain and in the valley. That kid there, in glasses, he's not in the mines yet, either. He used to sit behind me in class."

Honor and his friends have noticed the little boy, too. They tease him. Sneer at him. The boy ignores them . . . but that makes them mock him even more. The boy only squares his shoulders, pushes his glasses up on his nose, and stares straight toward the stage. Honor laughs.

I wish a monster would run out of the woods and growl at Honor, scare the smug expression right off his face. That'd be almost better than untold riches, seeing Honor Tumbrel put in his place.

Adam stands beside me. "Mr. Ramble," he says softly, tipping his hat.

I nod. "Mr. Peyton."

Thomp.

Thomp.

Thomp.

Someone climbs the stage from behind it with heavy footfalls. An excited *shhh* falls over the crowd.

A man strides onto the stage. His shiny black boots are eye level with us, so that's what I notice first. How glossy and clean they are. How they have no trace of coal dust. He wears black riding pants tucked into the boots. His burgundy coat is velvet, expensive, and perfectly fitted to his chest.

He saunters slowly across the planks, eyes sparkling as he looks us all over.

Then he smiles—straight white teeth, of course. That plus his jet-black hair—only slightly silver at the temples— make him look like a prince or a pirate from a book. He is handsome in a rugged, real kind of way. But there's no sadness marking his face, like there is on our faces.

"That's Mortimer Good," Adam whispers, with a hint of surprise in his voice.

My eyebrows rise so high that my hat pops up. "Really?"

Adam nods.

The Mortimer Good. The Head Guardian of the mountain and valley. I've always pictured Mortimer Good as some crabby old codger counting coins in the copper towers of his mansion. But this man looks dashing, brave, and young.

I glance at Adam again for confirmation. "You're sure?"

He nods again.

Mortimer's smile widens as he surveys the boys—plus me—waiting in the clearing.

I should hate Mortimer Good. If he's the head Guardian, he must know children are going Down Below. He must know about all the men, like my father, who are out of work, losing their voices, their sight, their lives. But . . . another part of me wants to know *him*. Wants to be close to him. Wants to impress him, maybe. This is the man who's slain more monsters than anybody, after all. He's a hero. A legend! Fear and excitement—and curiosity—they're twisted up so tight inside me right now that I can't pull them apart. What is he doing here? Why did he bring us?

Mortimer opens his arms wide, not like grannies do when they want a hug. But like he is about to put on some marvelous show.

"Welcome, brave gentlemen," he says, with a voice so deep it seems to burn through me. His voice is like the moonshine in Mama's cough medicine. "Destiny is waiting for some of you today. For the fearless among you. For those of you who are still brave enough to dream."

Flickering,

the Starpatch in my pocket.

Pounding,

the heart inside my chest.

I don't want to imagine any other place in the world as he speaks.

My heart is here, having a true adventure, I realize. I am one of those brave souls!

Soft rain begins to fall, teardrops tapping through the woods. Running down our faces. We're shivering. We're terrified. We're . . . excited.

"As you probably know, I'm Mortimer Good." Boys whoop and cheer, bursts of water splashing off all their clapping hands.

Mortimer waves away the cheers with a gracious smile. "Years ago, before you were even born, the Dust came and blotted out the stars. The magic we once knew seemed to be gone from our mountain. From our lives. But we pressed on, together. We forged a path through the mountain. And all of you have helped sustain that necessary way of life."

He pauses, takes a breath, and looks out over us like a proud parent. "And now our livelihood is being threatened again. That's why I need you, gentlemen, to be part of a special group I've decided to assemble. Dangerous missions lie ahead of you . . . if you even make it through today. But if you succeed, you won't just save your town. You'll save your family. You might even save yourself. Today, everything changes for you."

More roaring cheers all around me. I feel it, that energy that hope brings with it like a wave. My heart is fizzy with joy, even though I'm still afraid.

Adam does not cheer, though. Neither does the little boy with glasses. They both look soberly ahead. Even though they aren't showing the same excitement as the others, I can tell that they're captivated by Mortimer Good. We all are.

I haven't noticed the trees above us until this moment. How the empty branches reach for each other, stretch over us, connecting like a cage of bones. Their shadows make a spiderweb on the ground. And we are all standing here in it, I realize. All stuck now, in Mr. Good's shiny, starry web.

8

A Quest, Explained

Mortimer Good smiles down on us, proudly. The soft rain only makes him seem more mysterious, more handsome somehow. I've always heard of people capable of this: They walk into a room, and everybody turns to see them. They speak, and folks lean in and listen.

"Your fathers and mothers have worked hard to mine this mountain and make a life for you," Mortimer says, his voice carrying even through the ever-increasing rain.

"But the gold they've sought is running out. We're barely finding enough now. Of course, we've known for years that Forgotten Mountain isn't the only source for gold."

He was right; we all know the rhyme. *All tipped in gold, they call for thee.* The problem is that scaling these mountains is impossible.

"We've always thought the mountains are too difficult to climb. And that's true. But there's another way to the top. And it starts with brave dreamers, like you."

Gasps of disbelief rise from everyone. I look at Adam, and I know he's thinking the same thing: Mortimer Good has lost his mind. There is no way to the tops of those mountains. There's no way to avoid all the clouds of Dust we'd meet along the way.

"I hear you, boys!" Mortimer says, smiling at us. "Of course, I understand your concern. But there *is* a way to the top. No doubt about that. I wonder . . . do you have what it takes?"

The Guardians on the perimeter are among us now, passing out long ropes. Boys shove at each other to grab them. Adam hands one to me before snatching one of his own. I wish he'd stop trying to take care of me, but I'm also grateful. The rope prickles like hay in my hand; it's twisted and wet from the rain.

"What's this for?" I ask Adam. "Are we climbing?" I swallow nervously. Climbing the ladder to the loft in my house is hard enough with one hand. Climbing a rope up a mountain will be way more difficult.

Adam frowns, rubbing his thumb across his rope. "I don't know. I don't understand . . ."

Mortimer's eyes shine with something that looks like pride. "There *is* a way to the top of the mountains, boys. It's hidden here in the West Woods. You'll know it when you see it. Your mission today is to capture it and bring it back here. This is no easy task. But, if you prove yourself today, you'll begin a new chapter in our mountain's history."

Capture . . . *it*. I remember the scream from earlier— the same scream I heard that time in the woods. I feel a tightness across my shoulders; my heart drums a warning inside my chest.

"Adam." His name shoots out of my mouth as a burst, a frantic whisper. "Does he mean the monsters? Are we catching monsters?"

Adam doesn't answer, so I glance at his face, which has paled considerably. He's thinking the same thing I am. We aren't the only ones. Half the boys around us look nauseated. The other half shout questions at Mortimer Good:

"What do we catch?"

"How do we catch it?"

There's a dull roar in my ears as I imagine coming face-to-face with one of those things in the woods. It seems fitting, somehow. Our parents rode flying horses into a starry sky. We'll ride monsters through the Dust.

Mortimer raises his hands to silence us. "True courage comes in the unknown," he says. "You'll see soon enough."

"What's in it for us?" the small boy shouts. The crowd quiets at the sound of his voice. Because nothing about his voice is small. He's not rude or angry, but confident. Matter-of-fact. I like those traits. "The flyer says there's money involved."

Mortimer grins. "I'm a man of my word, gentlemen. Every boy who finds *it*—a way to the top—and brings it back here—will earn the chance of a lifetime. If you're brave enough to handle the adventure ahead, you'll earn a full thousand Feathersworth for every completed mission. And there are as many missions as there are mountains."

I feel like I'm staring but not seeing. Everything except Mortimer Good is a blur. He's spoken my daydreams into existence.

There are endless mountains. They stretch into forever.

Four missions equals four thousand Feathersworth.

That's it—four missions. I will have everything I need to save Denver . . . and then I can have more than I ever dreamed.

"This could be your new job," Mortimer says. "Before long, you'll make plenty for yourself, and for your families. You'll rid your family of their debt much faster than you would in the mines."

Rain slides down his face, outlining his sharp profile. His eyes are serious now, like they're searching our souls for true grit. "But this is not going to be easy, boys. So, here's your chance: Stay or go. I know it sounds like I'm describing a dream to you, but the path to get there is treacherous and difficult. Is it worth facing your fears to have what you want? You must decide now."

Some boys waste no time; they drop their ropes, turn, and leave the woods to head home. I understand why— the risk is huge. What if they get hurt just trying to prove themselves? Then they won't be able to work anywhere. No one teases them as they go, but they hang their heads anyway. I don't waver. Neither does Adam.

Because I remember a wish I made on a Starpatch: a wish for Denver to be healthy and happy and never ever afraid. No wasted years Down Below. No crows on the mountain. Nothing.

"All right, then," Mortimer says. He kneels down at the

edge of the stage, as if he's whispering in each of our ears: "You were never meant to waste away underground. You were meant for the skies. Ask yourself now: What is it you really want? If you work hard, you can have it. Starting today."

My heart thunders. I feel a fire inside me, licking at my bones.

I know what I want: Denver safe. Enough money to fix things. Debt's a heavy shadow hanging over all of us, and I want it gone. For good. Then Denver might really grow up—wild and free. Papa will be taken care of. Mama will rest her eyes against another mountain far away from here, one full of shining dreams and birdsongs. I will become a wild adventurer maybe. Go down into the mines; I'd find Papa's voice and catch it. Give it back to him.

Mortimer's Guardians are among us again, passing out bright red swatches of cloth. "Around the wrist," they calmly instruct. Our hands tremble as we tie.

"What in the world are these for?" Adam asks.

It's the little boy who answers us. He's moved close to us during the ruckus, and he reaches up to help me tie mine when he sees my Popsnap. Normally, I would pull away. I'm perfectly capable of doing this alone. But he's so nonchalant about it that I don't really mind. "I heard the Guardians over there talking," he says. "It's so they can see us if they have to go find us in the fog. Pull us out if . . . anything should happen." He tips his hat to me. "Greer Sutherland's the name, by the way." He glances from my face to Adam's. "I remember the two of you from school. I was a year below you."

Adam and I throw a sharp glance at one another. Greer knows I'm a girl. Will he give me away?

"Don't worry," Greer says, reaching to tie Adam's red cloth in place, too. "I can keep secrets." Adam's hands are trembling even worse than mine. His fingers are so thin and bony. The mines have turned my best friend into a walking skeleton.

"Good luck to you both," Greer says.

"Stick with us," I tell him softly. "Mountain kids stick together, no matter what. Right?"

Greer smiles gratefully and steps close to my side.

"Grab your ropes and climb onto the wagons!" Mortimer says. "And look up, boys! Look up! Why are so many of you looking at the ground today?"

We all do as he asks, almost all at the same time. We look up at the tops of the trees, heads tipped back to let the rain drip down our faces. I know why we look down: because we live in darkness. I keep my eyes down all day looking down at someone's floors, scrubbing someone's toilet, concentrating on the counter where I roll out stupid powder cakes. We look down because that's what we've learned. I live for the few minutes at the end of every day—at the beginning of every morning—when I get to look into the eyes of people I love.

They will be so proud of me, I remind myself.

I jump into the back of the wagon along with the other boys and feel Adam leap up quickly behind me. Greer after him. More boys from Coal Top clamber in after us. Glancing back, I see Mortimer, still on the stage. Beside him stands a figure that looks more like a tiny mushroom than a person—a kid with baggy brown clothes and a large brown hat on his head. There is no expression on the mushroom kid's face. But Mortimer is beaming, waving as we ride off into the woods. Mortimer Good is the first person I've seen in Coal Top in years with hope in his eyes.

The rain rolls over us in waves. Fog billows so thick around us, I lose sight of all other wagons. Chatter dies down in our cart. Everything is silent save the rain on the leaves, the creaking wheels of the wagons. The West Woods stretch for miles, over hills, past all sorts of bogs and ravines. There are plenty of paths along the way, and the wagons branch off, following those trails into the darkness. If rumors are true, these woods make their own paths sometimes, depending on whether they want people to stay . . . or leave.

Halfway up a steep ridge, our wagon slows. The Guardian driving drops his reins and looks back with a face as gentle and kind as an old grandpa's. "This is your stop, boys. Good luck to you."

And then a black-gloved hand grabs me by the shirt and I'm tossed off my seat, hitting the ground. Before I can even catch my breath, I'm shoved again, roughly, down a steep hillside. Fog so thick I can't see how far I'll go. How far I'll fall. Gasping for breath, I scramble for something to hold. But my boots and fingers slide through the never-ending slicks of mud.

"Mall—" Adam almost yells my name, nearly blowing my cover, that idiot—but his voice is suddenly silenced. And the silence feels like a punch in the heart.

"Adam!" I call out, unable to see anything. Or anyone.

The only response I hear is a scream.

9

Creatures

It's not Adam screaming, which is a small comfort. The scream fills my ears again, and I press my forearms against my head to muffle the noise.

That sound . . . it's the same sound I heard this morning at the boundary. And months ago when I was all alone, walking home in the night woods. I know it's a scream that doesn't belong to anything human. So,

I reach for the rope coiled a few feet in front of me and scramble in the opposite direction than the sound came from.

Footsteps snap somewhere close by me in the fog.

"H-hello?" I manage. I reach through the curtain of cold mist . . . thinking maybe someone's hand will touch mine.

And I take a step.

One more.

Reach . . . a little . . . farther . . .

Oof!

I trip on a tree root, staggering forward. Arms stretched long to brace myself, I slam into the wet, slimy bark of a tall tree. The trunk is cold and rough, but I rest my forehead against it anyway. Like it's a gentle giant, there to protect me.

I curl into it, try to make myself small against it.

Surely we're not catching monsters.

But what if we are?

What if it sees me before I see it?

How can I catch anything in a place where the step in front of me is barely visible?

I think of my father, how he always walks with his hands out, reaching, unfamiliar with the world he used to know so well. And then I picture Denver in the mines, trembling as he crawls deeper down.

Every muscle in my body wants to run. But if I run . . . I'll never make enough Feathersworth to save him.

I can save him.

Remember Denver, I tell myself.

He's always been my brave little burst of light, even when my heart was in a dark place. Sadness suffocates me sometimes. It presses against my heart and lungs and makes it hard to breathe. But Denver always lifts me out of that place, reminds me to choose joy. To fight for it, if it comes to that.

"Denver." I speak his name, because it gives me courage.

I imagine the feel of his dandelion hair against my chin when I hug him.

The warmth of him when I tuck him against me and read him stories.

I stand, my boots squishing a little in the thick mud around the tree.

I have no clue which direction to walk. But I know who I am walking for, and that's enough to push me deeper.

"Denver . . ." I say bravely.

And then that sound again—

Pop.

Crack.

And swissssssh *across the leaves.*

Maybe even a slither?

All the air feels forced from my lungs. My knees buckle, and I nearly tumble.

Footfalls, again, moving toward me.

I run—or I try to run, at least. One long stride, and I'm slammed by a wall of Dust so thick my eyes burn. My throat aches. I push my way to better air, clawing through the Dust, but the grit of it is sticky on my face.

I'll never get out. I'm alone in here. I'm lost, doomed. I'll be forgotten. Those thoughts are weights on my head, on my heart. I fling my arms to shoo the Dust away. The thoughts are worse in Dustclouds like this. Finally, it lifts, and I fall to my knees on the ground and breathe in the wet, musty air of the woods.

"Hello?" I squint through the fog ahead.

Nobody answers.

The movement continues, but now someone, or something, moves in a wide circle around me.

A slow stride.

A dragging step.

Swish . . .

Please let it be one of the boys, I think. Just some-one dragging his foot behind him. Someone injured in the fall.

"Adam?" I say, knowing it's definitely not Adam. Adam would already know it's me. He would call out if he was close.

"Who's there?" I demand, my breath disappearing into a cough.

This time, I get an answer . . . but it is not the one I want. The response to my question is a long, slow *hisssss* of delight.

And I run. I jump over tree roots and brambles.

Branches snap.

Boots stomp.

Muscles burn.

I slide, skidding downhill, scrambling to get away from whatever is tracking me through these cursed woods. I feel my Popsnap come loose and roll away—no! It's the best one I have, but I can't stop to find it. I race—into a deep grove of trees, where the fog is so thick that it clings to me, sticking like cobwebs against my face. I jump for a low branch, to climb a tree, but the bark is too slick and I can't grip it one-handed. I slam back against the ground with a hard *thud*. I let out a word that is not gentle. Mama wouldn't approve.

Too tired to run now, I jump up tall and hold my rope up high so the monster will see it.

As if a little rope will scare a monster, much less catch one. But it's all I can think to do.

Footfalls again . . . something circles me once more, stalking me from the thick of the mist where I can't see.

But . . . if I don't blink, I see something: a pale yellow fog swirling close to the ground.

Something is breathing . . . or slithering . . . just . . . there. There in that thick haze of Dust.

Sssss . . . the hiss fills me with dread. It's snakelike, and close to me.

And then I see it! Close to the ground, I see yellow eyes . . . two beady, bright yellow eyes with black slits in the center. The eyes are fixed on me. And they tilt, just slightly, as if the face belonging to those eyes is smiling. Delightedly.

I back up against the tree and slink to the ground. Cold sweat trickles down my face. My whole body shakes, fiercely.

I will never make it out of here. I'll never get out of the West Woods. I'll never get to tell Mama, Papa, and Denver how much I love them. Not to their faces, anyway.

"I love you Denver," I whisper. Fear has flattened most of my voice, but I had to get those words out. And I hope they float to him like a dream, like a Starpatch, one he can keep forever to think about me.

Suddenly, the air above me is shattered by wild flapping, a sound like like quilts snapping against the wind. *Huge* quilts.

Boom.

Something lands on the ground, shaking the earth all around me.

There is the unmistakable sound of a horse neighing wildly.

In my right mind, this might hit me as miraculous. But this minute, I'm so thrilled at the prospect of not being eaten by some giant fog-snake that I curl my knees close to my chest and watch.

Glimpses of the horse shine through the fog: the muscles on its hips flexing, moving, shimmering. The horse is black, sleek. Its gray hooves are larger than my head, snapping down with skull-splitting force against the ground.

The horse is trying to stomp that . . . thing.

I can see the thing, too; pieces of it, at least. Its tail whips around through the fog, sinister-looking, covered in sharp scales—the monster has to be nearly as big as the horse.

And the horse is *big*.

The monster screams.

I cover my ears. I press my body hard against the ground.

The horse rears back, then slams its front hooves down on the ground. It makes a screech of its own—a mighty roar of sound.

The monster runs away, slithering through the woods, the slimy tail whipping around, nearly grazing my ankle as it skids past.

The woods go quiet.

But I lie trembling.

I feel the horse watching me, even though I can't see its face. But I can see more of its shape now—more of its massive, muscular body.

"Thank you," I whisper, closing my eyes, wiping the mess of tears and snot off my face. The horse steps toward me, but this time its steps don't sound like an earthquake. They sound like soft, gentle thunder.

Very slowly, the horse lifts its hoof . . . and taps my

hand, which is still clutching the rope. I fling the rope away from me. I'd been holding it so tightly that it burned my hand, caused a long line of blisters right inside my palm. I press my hand flat against the cold mud. I know dirt's not good for a cut, but I'm desperate for some relief.

I flinch as I feel the horse's cold, soft muzzle touch the side of my face.

Get up now, it seems to gesture. *You're all right.*

My hand trembles as I reach to touch the horse's muzzle—its face is soft. Velvety as a blanket. I've never seen a horse this big or this gentle. I sit up, slowly, still mesmerized.

"Thank you for saving me."

The horse taps my forehead with its muzzle, like a quick kiss. Then it takes a few steps back, jerking its head—*follow me*—and trots off down the hill.

That's got to be my ride; the thought hits me like lightning. It makes sense, at least. Riding a wild horse up some dangerous mountain will be easier than riding a monster. I hope.

I follow the path the horse took and find it standing in a circle of bare trees nibbling grass.

As I move closer, fog rises from the ground like a curtain, catching in the treetops, finally giving me a full view of the creature who rescued me. The gray hooves.

The shiny black coat with starry white spots on the hips and . . .

A shocked sound—like a low scream—that I'm sure I've never made before escapes from my lungs. I shut my eyes tight. I must be dreaming this. *All* of this.

I open one eye . . . then the other. Joy, so full and wide that it's nearly suffocating, overwhelms me. Because this is no ordinary horse.

It has wings.

Wings! The wings are black, resting against its body.

This is a Starbird, just like the ones in the stories. For a moment, I wonder if I want this to be true so badly that I'm seeing things. We've been told they were gone. That they haven't been back in years. That they can't live here anymore, not beneath this Dust.

I step closer. Blink again. The wings don't disappear.

Another step.

The horse stops chewing. Regards me warily.

"May I?" I ask.

The horse remains still. I reach out and touch a feather on the wing—it feels like a leather fringe.

I am touching a flying horse.

A Starbird!

"You," I breathe, "are wonderwow." This, I realize, is not even a word. I wanted to say wow and I wanted to say wonderful and the words got smooshed together because I'm so happy. But it fits. This horse deserves his own word. A tingly, calm feeling rushes over me, followed by a nervous excitement that makes me want to squeal. Or sing. Or run. I can't wait to tell my family: The Starbirds are back!

This could mean all sorts of things, couldn't it?

If the horses are back, what if the light comes back, too? What if the Dust blows away somehow? What if we could get everyone out of the mines for good? As if to show off, the horse raises its head and stretches its wings out wide, just for me to see. The span is mighty.

I take a step back, trip on a tree root, and flop down on the ground.

The horse neighs . . . and it almost sounds like a laugh.

This *has* to be the way to the top that Mortimer was talking about. How did he know they're back? How did he find them with all these monsters crawling through the woods?

"I'm Mallie Ramble," I whisper.

The horse sizes me up with its big brown eyes.

And then it bows its face to me, an introduction. So . . . I stand. And curtsy. Then I lean closer, pressing my face to his. I'm not sure why I do this. I've never been around horses before. It's just instinct, I guess.

"I need your help," I tell it, softly. "I know we just met. And this is asking a lot. But I think you can help me if you'll"—I gulp—"come with me?"

The horse doesn't balk as I rest my left hand against its mane, lightly. *Steady*, I think. And I don't know if I'm thinking it for myself or for the horse.

"This way?" I ask.

The horse begins to walk beside me, slowly. Pace for pace. Just like friends are supposed to.

The woods seem quieter than normal but not in a scary way. In a reverent way. Like all the birds in these woods, all the creatures in the trees know this is a rare and magical creature walking.

We're near the clearing now; it felt so far away only a few minutes ago. But I hear a commotion up ahead, voices shouting. Horses neighing. My horse's muscles ripple under my hand as we move, and I feel bold.

Just as we're about to emerge into Mortimer's clearing, I pause in a shadow of trees. So does the horse. Instinct tells me to scope out the present situation before I burst in, so I take in the commotion ahead. The crowd from earlier has whittled down considerably. Since Mortimer offered us all a chance to go, boys have been leaving. More of them must have run for home as soon as they were dropped in the woods.

My eyes catch Adam's immediately, and my chest fills with relief. He's standing beside a tan, silver-winged horse. Adam's cut and banged up, but he looks okay otherwise. He didn't even lose his hat or scarf. Same with his friends— Nico, Connor, Wilder. None of them are on their horses, but their horses are all calm like mine. Nico made a bridle of the rope, which the horse doesn't seem to mind. Adam glances around frantically at the woods. Looking for me. The rest of the boys—including Honor Tumbrel—are trying to keep their horses from stomping them to bits. There are about twenty of us left, and we all have wild Starbirds.

The boys can't stop staring at the creatures. Neither can the men. I watch Connor reach out, gently, to touch his horse's gray-white wing. The horse bobs its head up and down, like it's saying yes. "Wow," the boy whispers. One of the Guardians sees this, too, and steps closer, trying to reach out and feel the wing the same way. But the horse snarls low, stomps its hoof, and scares the man away.

The little boy with the glasses—Greer—walks out of the woods nearest me with a horse in tow. He's not used a rope, either; his hand rests gently against the horse's leg. His Starbird is white, with gray spots. It towers over the boy protectively.

"Well done, lad!" Mortimer calls out to him.

My horse bangs his hoof against the ground, causing a boom of sound. He leads me out of the darkness, into the midst of the clearing. I follow, staying close to his side.

Everyone falls quiet—and so do the horses. They stare at my horse and me, eyes wide. Mouths agape.

"Dear Lord." One of the Guardians stumbles toward me. "She's caught a big one . . ."

"What?!" Honor Tremble shouts as he tries to reel in his horse. "Did you say *she*?! This isn't a job for girls."

And then he whirls around and sees me. His face flames red with anger. Eyes flicker with rage. "Especially *that* girl."

My gaze locks with Adam's, and I see more fear in his eyes than I've seen all day. He's afraid I'll get booted now. I am, too. He's looking at my hair, the telltale proof I haven't followed the rules of the flyer.

I hadn't realized it till now; my hat is gone. Lost somewhere in the woods. My hair has come loose from the braid, and it's falling long, dark, and frazzled all around me. The boys all stare at me, some with disgust, because I'm a girl and I'm here. Some with curiosity—because my right arm doesn't have a Popsnap attached. As if that's a bigger deal than a flying horse. And some boys—like Honor—level me with a cold glare.

"That's Mallie Ramble." Honor spits my name. "She's a maid in the valley. She's a filthy mountain girl. Get rid of her! That's against the rules."

"The flyer says young fellers only!" shouts one of Honor's cocky friends.

"Everyone calm down." Mortimer's voice is steel, closer behind me than I realized. The hair on my neck rises. My horse and I swerve to look at him.

Mortimer stares at me, and I wonder if he's sizing me up. Deciding. I can't tell if it's delight or fury in his eyes.

"She's no wiry young feller," Mortimer says finally. "But she certainly looks brave."

I turn loose a breath I didn't realize I was holding.

Mortimer doesn't glance at my right arm. Not once. And he doesn't look at my long hair. I feel like he's seeing me—the heart of me—and deeming every part of me capable. A kind, wide grin stretches over his face. "This is my plan, after all. What I say goes. And I say . . . welcome, Mallie Ramble."

And I know in my heart, as sure as I've known anything, that this is the beginning of something grand.

10

Rules of Play

"Everyone try to stay calm," Mortimer tells us. "Starbirds are surely like any other horse; they sense your feelings. If you're scared, they'll be scared."

Calm. How is it possible to be calm in a situation like this? The boys around me must all feel the same way. Their chests are heaving with excited breaths.

"I still don't think it's fair," Honor mumbles.

"Actually, this is more fair, isn't it?" Mortimer asks Honor. "Here's one of your first great life lessons, young men. And woman." He nods to me. "The person who makes the rules can change the rules. I made this rule. I choose to change it. And let's be honest now. The flyer said orphans were preferred. How many of you are orphans?"

Silence.

The boys all glance at each other. Only a few raise their hands. I narrow my eyes at Honor, waiting to see if he'll lie his way into a spot. But he only stands up straighter, sword clutched, jaw clenched, glaring at me. I feel sorry for his horse.

Mortimer smiles. "I asked for orphans because these missions are so dangerous. I thought orphans would be the most fearless, with nothing to lose. I suppose I under-estimated how brave you boys can be." He turns to me, again. "And clearly, I underestimated what young women on Forgotten Mountain are capable of doing."

Pride roars inside me again. I wish Mama and Papa could see this. I wish Denver could see this.

Mortimer walks to Greer's horse, pats the animal's spotted hip. I notice my horse snorts as Mortimer passes us.

My horse. Already, I want this creature in my life. Need him. Already, he belongs to me. Which means I need to give him a name other than *horse*.

"So many people believed all the Starbirds were gone forever," Mortimer says, running his fingers down the horse's muzzle. "But I'd heard rumors that some remained. That some were trapped here in the woods."

He circles back to the center and speaks to all of us. "Most of the Starbirds left when the Dust came, barred forever by that wretched wall of Dust. That's true. But there've been sightings off and on ever since. And as our resources grew scarce, I thought about how wonderful it would be if those stories were true—if some of the horses remained. They helped us years ago, when we needed them. Perhaps they'd help us again. The Guardians have searched the woods for years, but Starbirds are elusive creatures. And then it occurred to me—we weren't sending the right people to look. These horses love children. And I asked myself: What if, when the children all left to go into the mines and into the valleys, that's why Starbirds became so scarce? If children braved the monster woods to find them, would they come for you?"

He turns a circle in the clearing, looking over the mighty creatures that've come out of hiding. "I was right, of course. You proved it. You stepped into the woods, and they came to you!"

We could have been eaten by monsters in the process, I think. But I don't say anything.

He smiles at the rest of us. "And now for the best part of my plan. You're going to learn to fly on these Starbirds. And then you will collect gold from the mountaintops we thought we couldn't reach. Gold powder is thick on the tops—just waiting to be harvested. And then, maybe, the mines will become obsolete. It's a shame, an embarrassment, that we send children to the mines. That we have to send boys down there in the prime of their lives . . ."

Mortimer keeps talking, but his words become a far-away echo. I can't concentrate on anything beyond this one wild promise:

You're going to learn to fly on these Starbirds.

My knees feel wobbly all of a sudden, and I lean hard into my horse's side to keep from flopping down on the ground. I'm going to fly? Yesterday morning, I was knee-deep in muck cleaning floors . . . and now I'm going to learn to fly?

Mortimer signals to two of his men, and a giant fabric tapestry unfurls—stretched between the treetops. The tapestry is a map—simple, inky black mountains painted against the beige. My horse leads me closer to get a better look. Forgotten Mountain is the first one on the map. But there are other peaks—many peaks—rippling far out, far past us, all the way to the edges. The nearest ones we memorized as kids: Mount Carson, fierce and pink; the Pembers, always covered in snow. The Lightning Range, full of ever-changing weather. Mirror Mountain, covered in ice so thick you can see a perfect reflection of the sky.

"Here is where you are." Mortimer gestures to the first mountain—to the West Woods of Forgotten Mountain. "Beyond those woods are more vast and beautiful—and very, very magical—mountains. Some you've heard of. Others, far away from here, no one has even traveled. But every mountain has gold powder near the top; we've always known that. Your mission is simple. Fly to the mountain, obtain the gold powder, and bring it back to me. Fill your bag with gold powder on every ride and you'll get a thousand Feathersworth."

Four rides.

That's all it would take to pay off our debt!

"Before you get too excited," Mortimer continues, "know that it's not as easy to harvest gold powder as you think. You'll have to learn to ride a flying horse, for start-ers. You'll have to deal with the elements, maybe even with . . . creatures like you saw today. You'll have to learn to fly as high as possible, while avoiding dangerous clouds of Dust."

"I could fight a monster," Honor shouts. "I'm a trained swordsman."

I snort. *Trained swordsman.* Sword fighting is a popular sport in the valley. Girls aren't allowed to compete, of course. But sometimes, during breaks, we meet in the alleys and sword practice with broomsticks. Just because they won't give girls swords doesn't mean we don't know how to fight. And I'd bet a thousand Feathersworth that we're more talented with sticks than Honor Tumbrel is with a blade. He couldn't fight his own shadow.

"Let's hope you don't have to try," Mortimer says, clapping his hands together to change the subject. "You've had a full day, brave riders. If you want to accept this challenge, then come back tomorrow after your work is through for the day. We'll have a quick riding lesson and set off for our first mission."

Adam pulls off his cap. Pushes his hands through his hair. His cheeks flame scarlet, which doesn't happen when he's embarrassed. He's frustrated. "A quick practice? Shouldn't it take a few weeks, at least, to learn this?"

"You'll learn to trust your horses," Mortimer says mysteriously. "They'll know what to do. And I'll be here to help you. We can only live the stories we're given. "That's an old saying in the valley and on the mountain. We can only live the stories we're given. I've never cared for that way of thinking. It makes it sound like nothing can be changed. And maybe some things can't. But . . . What if? "Now," Mortimer says after a breath." Here's the story I'm giving you: Ride for me and save your town, or . . . go back to where you were. And wait for someone to save you."

I clench my jaw, resolved. My heart is decided. If there was a question of this—who would rescue and who would be the rescuer—I want to be the hero.

I'll be Mallie over the Moon.

I can't stop babbling to Adam about all we've seen as we stomp back home through the woods. My mind is a river of words and thoughts, and I let them flow freely.

I tell him about the monster that came after me, and the moment I saw my horse—and realized what my horse actually was.

"A Starbird, Adam! Can you believe it? Do you know what this could mean? What if there's a way through this Dust? What if it's . . . I don't know . . . breaking up or something?"

Adam remains silent.

We're nearly back to the platform in Coal Top when he finally speaks up. "The farther we get from the West Woods, the more it all feels like a dream."

I know what he means. Coal Top looks exactly the same as always: dusk and darkness and drooping pines. Dustblobs in the trees. More gray Dust blowing through the streets. But if I close my eyes, I can still feel my horse's soft hair underneath my hand. The way my heart twinged when the Guardians guided them back into the West Woods. The horses didn't like that, but they obeyed. At least, I think they did.

What if my horse isn't there when I return tomorrow?

"Something doesn't feel right," Adam finally says.

I raise my eyebrows. "Nothing feels right. There's no guidebook for this. We're about to ride flying horses and collect gold powder from the mountaintops. How do you know what that's supposed to feel like?"

"I don't trust Honor Tumbrel or his friends on land, much less the sky. We have to watch our backs."

"Watch each other's backs."

As we climb down the ridge toward the depot, we see two people waiting on the platform: Granny Mab and Greer.

She rests her old hands on the small boy's shoulders. "Is it true, Mallie?" Her voice breaks over the words, the way hope does when it's stretched to its limit. "Did you see the . . . the Starbirds?"

"It's true," I tell her.

Mab is not the crying sort. She's a tough old bird. But tiny tears glisten down her wrinkly face. "I can't believe it," she says. "I hoped, of course. But . . . wow."

Wonderwow, I think. "I can't wait to tell Mama."

"Looks like you won't have to wait," Adam mumbles, and he points to the boundary line for the North Woods. Mama is standing there, hands on hips. But her eyes aren't full of pride. Just fury.

11

Explanations

The cottage door slams behind me. Papa, Denver, and Honeysuckle all turn their heads toward the sound.

"I don't understand why you're angry," I say to Mama, nearly shouting. "This is a good thing. It's kind of a miracle!"

"This is dangerous! An absolute terror! How do you think I felt when the Tumbrels sent a servant looking

Denver cocks his head, confused. "Mallie didn't go to the valley?"

"No," I answer. "I went to the West Woods."

His eyes go wide as I step toward him, kneeling down on the ground so I'm in front of him and Papa. So they're listening closely.

"There are Starbirds still in the West Woods," I tell them. "Just like in the old stories! Mortimer Good thought they might be there—and he was right! The horses thought all the children had left, when we went into the mines and valley. But they know now that we didn't. Do you know what that means? The Starbirds can help us again. They can carry us to the top of the far mountains to harvest gold."

"Us?" Denver raises his eyebrows hopefully. "Like, me and you?"

Papa instinctively locks his arm tight around my brother. Then he reaches out for me.

"Just me, for now," I say, taking Papa's hand. "Me and the older kids. This means you can stay in school. And I can pay off our debt. You don't have to worry about the mines anymore."

I might be talking to Denver, but I'm saying it loud enough for Mama and Papa to hear me.

"You have never been on a horse," Mama says. "Not the kind that roams on land. Not to mention a Starbird! This is dangerous, Mallie. What if you get hurt on one of these missions? Then there's no way out of this! We have a plan in place. You work; we save money—"

"But never enough money," I insist.

Her eyes soften. She knows it's the truth. I'm not even good at math, but I know we could never save up on land what I could make in the sky.

"If something happens to you . . ."

"Nothing will happen to me," I assure her. "Mountain people used to ride all the time—"

"I know about the Starbirds," Mama says. "But that was a long time ago. Things are different now."

"Exactly!" I nod. "Things are different. We have to find different ways to do things. I can do this. I won't get hurt. I promise. And otherwise, everything will be the same. I'll keep going to the valley. Keep earning money from the Tumbrels, too. But after work . . . I'm doing this. For all of us. I don't understand why you aren't happy. This is like a fairy tale, Mama."

"Nothing is a fairy tale when Mortimer Good is involved," Mama warns me. And she says nothing else for the rest of the night.

12

Girl with a Green Stripe

Sometimes when a mighty event befalls your life—be it a tragedy or something wonderful—it's hard to tell when you're dreaming or awake.

Was I dreaming last night? When a monster stalked me in the darkness? When a Starbird rescued me in the woods? When my mama—too angry to even speak— marched me back home?

Or did I, Mallie in the Muck, find a Starbird in the West Woods?

I wake to a room that looks the same as always. There's the shelf of the few books I own, which I've read over and over. The stuffed bear I sleep with is still in my arms. My wall has two sketches on it—one of my family, all together, Honeysuckle perched on Dad's shoulder (Adam crushed a dandelion petal against the page to give her color). And the picture of a daisy bundle that Adam drew for me a few years ago. All of that is the same.

But in my heart, I feel like a different person.

I close my eyes to stretch and hear a soft chirp.

"Hi, Honeysuckle," I whisper. Opening one eye, I see a blurry swipe of yellow on the small table beside my bed. Honeysuckle watches me carefully with her sweet brown eyes.

"You should have woken me up earlier."

The bird hops onto my bed, up to my pillow. She stretches one sunny wing and touches a scratch on my face with the tip of her feather.

"I'm okay," I whisper again.

Feathers. I think about the feel of feathers.

The Starpatch felt like that, like a bird's feather.

But the feathers on the horse's wings felt different—leathery and strong, made to ride a storm, snap a thundercloud in half. I'll know how that feels soon. I'll be a rider.

Mallie over the Moon.

I stand slowly, and Honeysuckle bounces onto my shoulder.

Careful steps through the gauzy-dark room.

Fingers fumble around on my table until I find a match-box. Leaning down, I hold the box still with my right arm.

Snap.

Hissss.

> *A burst of flame on the edge of the match*

> *and my lantern is lit.*

I'm not usually the kind of girl who stares at herself in a mirror. Once you've had one good look at your face for the day, I figure that's enough. But today is different. I have to make sure I look the same after everything that's happened. I wipe the dust from my mirror.

Mostly, yes.

Freckles like my papa's.

Eyes like my mama's.

"Is she still mad at me?" I ask softly so I don't wake Denver.

The bird whistles low and long. That's a yes, for sure.

I thought she would be proud of me. But she was furious—she didn't even say good night!

I pull my hair around to brush through the tangles and gasp—

A flash of green catches my eye.

Green?

My eyes widen in the mirror as I lean closer.

"Oh . . . my."

A bright green stripe is shining in my hair. Starting from the roots on the right side of my head, and sparkling, emerald-shimmery, all the way to the tips. Now, if I were a girl from Windy Valley, this might be a grand thing. I would have gone to a caretaker to have this specific shade mixed for me—probably from some dangerous mineral that grows in the mines. But I am not that girl; I'm a mountain girl, and I did nothing to my hair yesterday.

A soft knock on the door, and Mama's peeking inside.

"What's this?" I whisper.

She takes the long green stripe between her fingers.

"Did I step in a cursed creek in the West Woods?" I ask.

When I was a girl Mama liked to tell that story, of a

cursed creek in the West Woods that'd turn your hair white or green or blue or yellow. I've always thought it was a fairy tale. Now I know anything can be true.

She shakes her head. "Your horse marked you," she says. "Next time you see your ride, you'll see he has the same color in his hair as you do. That's what happens when you connect."

I cock my head at her, feel my eyebrows squish together. "How do you know that?"

"I remember them," she says. "I remember when they were here."

I reach out and grip her hand in mine. "They're here again, Mama," I say. "Why aren't you happy? Why aren't you excited?"

"Because I want you safe."

"I will be safe," I whisper. "And then we'll be out of debt. I'll work and ride and pay off everything—"

"Mallie," she says, interrupting me. Maybe this is it—she'll tell me she's proud of me. That she'll help me, all she can. "We'll talk about this at breakfast."

So I wait.

Ms. Marcia's apple puffs are in a pile in the center of the table. I'm hungry enough to gobble up each one, but I make myself go slow.

Denver stares at my green stripe.

Finally, Mama says, "I don't trust Mortimer Good, Mallie. Those horses left for a reason, and I just . . . I want you to be very wary when he's around. Plus, back in the day, those horses helped us harvest starlight. Something about snatching up gold . . . that doesn't sit right in my heart."

I nod. "I understand what you're saying. But we've got to survive on something, right? This is a thousand Feathersworth per mission. Mama . . . that's enough to change things. And maybe we'll have *enough* gold powder eventually. Enough for everybody."

"When it's gold powder you're talking about," she says, her face eclipsed by a chipped teacup, "there will never be enough."

"I'm going to take care of us, all of us," I promise her. "Haven't you ever wanted to do something brave?"

Her eyes bore into mine and I see the hurt in them.

"I didn't mean it that way," I clarify quickly. "You're brave for us all the time. Let me be brave for us, too."

There's a sad pause as she looks down at her apple puff, the clang of a fork against a cracked plate.

"I want to see you ride!" Denver's voice erupts in the silence.

"No!" Mama and I both shout it. Honeysuckle gives one defiant chirp.

"*You* hide today," I tell Denver. "Remember those men

who came looking for you? They might come back. So you have to hide until I have all the Feathersworth we need. Got it?"

He nods, propping his head on his hand with a sigh. "Yeah."

Mama rises suddenly. She walks to the back door of our cottage, and the burst of cold is so icy it nearly takes my breath away. She keeps an old chair out back—a thinking place, she calls it. I know that's where she's going. But I don't know why. There's nothing to think about now. There's plenty, however, to be grateful for.

"I don't understand why she's so angry."

Papa doesn't answer me. He can't answer me. But he reaches for the notebook he keeps close and scribbles messy sentences for me to read:

Trust your horse.
Trust your heart.
Love.

I stand and lean over to kiss Papa's head. But he grabs my hand and holds it, tight. "I love you, too," I whisper. And I bolt out the door.

13

Powder Cakes

The Tumbrel mansion stands on the highest hill in the valley. There are two tall windows in the front, from the base all the way to the rooftop. And on days like this, when we have the Dust and dark, rainy skies to deal with, lanterns beam from the dead center of those windows. They look like beacons in the Dust. Eyes in the darkness. I'm late this morning; it took ages for me to find my other Popsnap buried deep in a trunk of clothes I've outgrown. It doesn't fit very well, I realize as I try to adjust it for the hundredth time. But it will have to do. Thankfully, nobody has noticed the time.

Carriages line the cobblestone walkway to the house. A party has been in progress all night. Valley people don't plan parties that last for an hour or two. They spend full days—sometimes a full week—celebrating. And anything merits a celebration for them. I sigh at the scene playing out in the windows.

Wax drips down the chandeliers I cleaned. Powder cakes that took hours to make are being thrown by Mrs. Tumbrel's rotten kids. Honor and his friends are running up and down the stairs in black capes, clashing swords, pretending to fight. All day, on every floor, adults will arrive and drink from silver mugs, heads tilted back in laughter. Or they'll be passed out on couches and stairways throughout the mansion. I wonder if the Tumbrels threw this party because the Starbirds are back.

But when I slip inside, no one is mentioning the horses at all. They're toasting Honor's father, who has been promoted to Head Guardian of the valley mine.

I slip into the kitchen. If this really works out—flying horses around to the mountaintops—I can eventually leave the Tumbrels for good. But eventually isn't today. So my plan is to do even more work than usual to ensure I get paid something for the week.

The thought of someday still adds a sure-footed boldness in my steps, though. Today, I'll be knee-deep in dirt. But this evening, I will be flying through the skies, saving my little brother from a future in the mines. Yesterday, I only hoped for change. But this is better than anything I could have hoped for.

I pull the slop bucket and mop to the middle of one of the bedroom floors to start my chores. I'm smiling, actually *smiling*, because I know as soon as this is done I'm riding horses. My horse. I'm riding a Starbird!

Before I even realize what I'm doing, my finger's drawing stars in the dust. Mama and Papa told me what the stars look like: round centers. Shiny spikes. A thousand different colors. *And the stars tell stories*, Papa told me once. *Trace the colors and you'll find shapes of hundreds of different creatures. A bear. A whale. A lion.*

"Leo," I whisper, drawing the pattern of freckly stars I saw on my horse's hip yesterday. It is the name of the star lion in one of Papa's tales. I can't wait to tell my horse that it's his name, too.

"Green is a terrible color on you." Honor Tumbrel stands in the doorway, one foot propped over the other. He looks the same as he did yesterday in the forest: new clothes, new boots, fine jacket, polished sword. I'm in old rags with my hair tied back. Honor has a streak of blue swiped through the blond across his forehead.

He fiddles with the silver buttons on his sleeves, grinning. "My mom asked for a hundred more powder cakes. I'd get started on those immediately, if I were you. Then you can finish up these floors and my laundry, and, best of all"— he smirks—"you can polish the chandelier in the kitchen."

I anticipated this, all of it. I knew he would pick the chores that took the longest today.

"I'll still be at the mission," I tell him. "No matter how much you give me, I'll be there."

"We'll see," he says, and he watches silently while I begin my work.

Powder cakes are a special kind of terrible. They're two inches high, two inches around, and must be the exact same shape each time. The sugar dusted over the top must be the exact same thickness on every single one. They're a waste of time and taste awful, but valley people love them. One time I made them, I used salt instead of powder on top. While I got my point across, the incident got me fired and landed me with the Tumbrels.

So, for over an hour, I pound out powder cakes and place them in equal rows on the gleaming kitchen counters

I just cleaned. Then I spin into the cupboard for more flour to make a second batch.

"Congratulations, Otis!" I hear someone say in the next room. Through a wide slat in the pantry I see them all: the adults shaking hands, congratulating one another. Men in capes. Women in fussy velvet dresses. Their screeching laughter always makes my head hurt. Otis, Honor's father, shakes the man's hand. "Grateful you could come and celebrate, friend!"

"Of course!" the man says. "And young Honor will follow in your footsteps in no time. I see you've already bought him a sword."

Otis chuckles deeply and sips from his copper cup. "Honor can barely hold a sword. Much less fight with one."

I agree with this statement completely.

"The Starbirds," the other man says quietly. "You think . . . it's a good idea?"

I strain to hear what Otis says. This is the first I've heard of the horses all day! But the music has swelled up again, and people are dancing in circles, kicking up the Dust that's crept through open windows and doors.

"Time will tell," Otis replies. He mumbles something I can't hear—mumble, mumble—and then, ". . . Mortimer."

The other man curves so his shoulder is to the crowd and says something low that I can't make out. I wish I could train Honeysuckle to swoop in and spy for me. ". . . you know to use this sparingly," the man says. "You know to use this well."

The man hands over a small sack, tied in plain twine. Otis peeks inside, and I see a hint of dull yellow powder. At first, I think it's gold powder, but no—gold has a shine to it. This is more like the powder Adam pointed out in the West Woods. Otis bows his head in gratitude and tucks the bag into his coat.

I take my bag of flour, silently, and step back into the kitchen to work.

Once the powder cakes are all done, I wipe my forehead and get started on the kitchen floor.

Which takes a long time since Honor keeps coming to "check on me" and drag his boots all across it.

I hear his heavy footfalls walk in the door now—a third time—and I swirl around, throwing my dirty rag at his shoe as hard as I can.

"Watch it!" he shouts. "If you ruin these boots, you'll buy me new ones."

And then I smile. I can't help it. "You're afraid I'm going to beat you. That I'll be a better rider than you."

He laughs. "Not remotely, Mallie in the Muck. And sadly, I won't even get to see you try." He pulls the timepiece from his pocket and holds it up for me to see. It swings in the light with a hypnotic shine. The smile slides off my face now. I didn't realize how late it was . . .

"Because you can't ride if you don't know how. And you have too much work left to do to make it to practice. I'm headed up the mountain now. Should I tell them not to expect you today?"

My heart sinks. I haven't paid attention to the dimming of the sky. I've been working too hard trying to finish everything! "I'll be there," I say as I set my jaw and climb the ladder to get started. Honor walks away laughing. Honeysuckle—my bright yellow beacon of hope—darts through the open window and settles on the chandelier.

"I'm supposed to be in the clearing," I tell her, through clenched teeth. And yet, as always, I'm Mallie in the Muck—perched on top of a rickety ladder, pulling candle wax from crystals on a chandelier. Piece by piece. There are hundreds.

"I'll never wear a piece of jewelry made of a cave crystal," I mumble.

Honeysuckle chirps once in total agreement.

Cave crystals are a grisly red color, and each one makes a faint screeching sound if you barely even touch it. But I work carefully to clean each one.

I feel every second.

Every minute that stretches . . .

Honeysuckle flaps over to the top of a blue china cabinet, bouncing anxiously. Time is running low . . .

"Last one," I promise her. My fingers are throbbing now.

I freeze as I hear high-heeled boots climbing the steps. Mrs. Tumbrel is coming to find me. Honeysuckle is chirping, bouncing. I know what she's trying to say: *Run. Go. She'll find more for you to do!*

I bound down the ladder, store it, and run and hide behind the door. She'll definitely see me here, but there's nowhere else I can hide.

"Mallie!" Mrs. Tumbrel calls my name.

Through the crack in the door, I see Honeysuckle bite a flour bag on top of the pantry, which spills in a waterfall of white on Mrs. Tumbrel. I can't wipe the smile off my face as I scramble quietly out the door, Honeysuckle flapping along behind me.

I run for the West Woods, where I belong.

14

Mount Carson

"Where've you been?" Adam shouts as I sprint up to the edge of the clearing. His sleeves are cuffed, and his cheeks are red; he's been riding. They've all been riding. I'm so far behind.

"I waited as long as I could for you at the boundary," he says, scampering along beside me. "What took so long? And why are you gripping your elbow?"

"Where's Leo?" I ask, running ahead of him. Drops of sweat trickle down my forehead and sting my eyes. I can barely get any words out of my chest. I'm not remotely worried about my arm, which is just a little sore from wearing the old Popsnap. What I'm worried about is the fact that I'm late on day one of horse flying practice.

Because I'm assuming flying isn't something that comes naturally. A little practice *would* be nice.

"Who's Leo?" Adam asks, confusion in his voice.

"My horse," I tell him as I jog toward the horses. "My arm is fine." I run toward the ruckus of sound ahead of me. The winged horses are all clustered together in the middle, standing in a half circle against the tree line. They're stomping their mighty hooves against the ground, flapping their wings. The flapping sound is what sends wonderful shivers down my spine; it's like they're slicing the wind in half. It's like they are the wind.

The horses are all different colors: black, tan, gray, silvery white. Some of their wings are plain, the same color as their hair. Others have wings with patterns of wild, glorious colors. But I can't find *my* horse.

"Am I too late?" I ask breathlessly. "Did I miss the mission?"

"No," Adam says, his voice softening. "But you did miss the entire riding lesson. It's been pandemonium, so

120

nobody's going to notice you were gone. Iggy's going to bring Leo, and maybe she'll give you the highlights."

"Who is Iggy?"

"She's one of Mortimer's helpers. Just stand here for a second, Mallie. Take some deep breaths. The horses can sense it if you're fired up."

I can see that this is accurate. Everyone is in a frenzy trying to get their horses saddled and bridled. The horses clearly haven't done this in a while. In ever, maybe. Did the Weavers use saddles long ago? I don't know. Neither do the Guardians. They look as confused as the riders when it comes to saddling a flying horse. They must not have lived on the mountain back when the Starbirds were here. They don't know how to treat them.

Some boys have managed to walk beside their horses, calming them. I notice now they all have a new twist of color in their hair. We've all been marked by our rides.

"Where's Mortimer?" I ask Adam.

"Not here yet. I'm not worried about him. I'm worried about you."

I realize that I'm gripping my arm again. I let go, quickly.

"Well, I am worried about falling off my horse mid-air," I say. "And don't say anything to anybody about my arm, okay? Just don't point it out. The other day, all those guys wanted me to leave because I was a girl. Mortimer didn't seem to care about that. I don't want him to think the arm is an issue. I don't want people to feel sorry for me and I don't want people to be inspired because I wear a Popsnap. I just want to ride—"

"Hey." His voice softens. "I didn't mean to get you worked up. It's called concern. Friends are allowed to be concerned for each other. Have I ever taken it easy on you because one arm is shorter than the other?"

I grin. "Nope. I like that you haven't. I just wish this orange Popsnap wasn't the first thing people notice about me."

"Well, it might be." Adam shrugs. "People notice I'm tall. That's always what they see first. I can't change that. If they talk to me for more than a few minutes, they know it's just one of a zillion traits that make me . . . me." He cocks his head and points to the Popsnap. "I thought you lost it in the woods?"

"I have an extra one," I tell him. "An old one." *That hurts like the dickens*, I think.

"Do you think it will be hard to ride with a Popsnap?"

"Yesterday it was just hard, period—and we weren't even riding yet. I don't know if the Popsnap mattered. The only thing I'm worried about is the reins. How to hold them, how to steer."

Adam chews on his lip, thinking. It's like watching

him work out a math problem back at school. "Iggy can help with that."

I want to know how this *Iggy* knows so much about Starbirds but something distracts me before I can ask.

"Hey," I say, reaching for the twist of silver in his hair. "This is new. It looks cool."

"Not as cool as yours," he says. He reaches for my green stripe of hair, pulls it through his fingers. I know he's only touching my hair because it's suddenly *green* green, grassy green. But I can't help the flutter inside me when he does it. His face reddens and he drops my hair, stepping back.

Seeing Adam with a twist of silver hair makes me wonder what he will look like as an old man. Will we still be friends when we're old? Will we talk about this moment— these days—when we flew on wild horses side by side?

I clear my throat and look away. "If this Iggy person doesn't bring my horse, I'm going to go find him myself."

"No need," Adam says, tapping my arm. He points toward the tree line of the clearing. Leo's running toward me, looking even more beautiful than he did yesterday. His shiny black coat. His leathery wings. Every horse here looks different, but Leo is the most beautiful. Some wings have patterns on them, bright as butterflies. Some look painted, with spots and star shapes. But Leo's wings are dark and shiny. The color of water at night. *The color of magic*, I think.

Leo is ready for riding—or flying, I guess. He's saddled, with a bridle. And even though he's massive, I hold out my arms like I'm waiting for a puppy to jump up into them. He calms when he's close enough for me to hug his soft neck.

"Leo," I say softly.

I pull back, and his gentle brown eyes meet mine, his wings folded against his back. He leans low, touching his velvety nose to my forehead. "Hi," I say. "Do you like your name okay? Leo?"

Leo closes his eyes, then nudges my forehead with his muzzle, like a kiss. My heart melts at the sight of the green stripe glimmering in his mane. I've heard about girls in Windy Valley who give ribbons to their friends—rare silky ribbons, sewn with diamond thread. They wear the same color so people know they're connected. Now Leo and I have matching stripes in our hair. We're connected, him and me.

I rub the soft skin of his nose, and he closes his eyes in happiness. "I came up with your name because of your freckles," I whisper. "The freckles on your sides—they look like the Leo constellation. My papa says the Leo constellation is shaped like a lion. I think you are lionhearted, too. I think you're brave."

"I would say you're both that way." Mortimer Good is standing behind me. He's wearing another fine suit today: black velvet jacket, pants with silver side stitches, and shiny riding boots. And he's wearing a dashing grin, which makes me smile nervously in response.

Mortimer reaches for the green strand of hair framing my face. "I see the horse has marked his rider. He won't let anyone else get on his back now."

"I named him Leo."

Mortimer smiles. "Call him whatever you like. You've got more to worry about than names. Remember what you learned from Iggy so you don't kill yourself up there."

I gulp and nod. The problem, of course, is that I haven't learned anything from Iggy.

As Mortimer strides away, he says, "Give Miss Ramble her Keep, Iggy."

At first, I see no one behind Mortimer. Then someone clears their throat, and I look down.

Iggy—I'm assuming this is Iggy—is the same person I saw with Mortimer the day we rode into the woods. Standing no more than three feet tall, she wears all brown—baggy pants, jacket full of pockets, slouchy brown boots. Her hair is tucked up into a brown knit hat on her head. Iggy's not a rider, but she's clearly familiar with horses. I can see by the way she reaches for Leo, no fear at all. He nuzzles into her small hand. Plus, she's clearly respected by Mortimer. I have a feeling that earning his respect is a big deal. Maybe we could stick together, us girls. I wonder if she's as happy to see me as I am to see her.

Iggy doesn't make eye contact. She points to my shoes. "No riding boots, I see."

"Just work boots." Does anybody have riding boots? Did anybody have time to change after work? I doubt it.

"Won't be easy," Iggy says. "Flying in a dress."

"I didn't have time to change," I admit. My cheeks are warm with embarrassment. I'm doing the best I can, and I don't enjoy these reminders about how unprepared I am. I don't know why Iggy is even mentioning all this. "I'll make it work. I'm Mallie, by the way."

"I know who you are. Here's your Keep. This is the sack for your gold powder. Hooks to your belt. When you spy some gold, unhook the Keep, scoop up what you can. Give it an easy shake and it'll sift out any dirt, debris, or pigeon poo you happen to collect accidentally. Any questions?"

Yes! I want to shout. But I say, "Could you maybe, um, go over the highlights again? Of how to fly?"

Iggy finally looks up at me like she's thoroughly annoyed. She has one brown eye and one that's the brightest blue. She's very pretty, I think. Also, she has a very crabby attitude. "I won't tell Mortimer you were late," she says softly. "But I don't give special lessons to latecomers, either."

Any hope of friendship I've been holding flies out the window. I wonder if Leo will snort at her, the way he did at some of Mortimer's men yesterday.

He doesn't.

Leo leans down and nuzzles her face. That traitor.

For the first time, a smile quirks the edge of her tiny mouth.

"Be good to this horse," she says, turning up her nose and marching away. "Trust him and you'll be fine."

"Gentlemen!" Mortimer calls. "And lady." He bows to me. Some of the boys laugh. "It's time for your first mission. Mount your horse, if you haven't already, and ride to the edge of the cliff just over that rise."

Easy enough, I think. I tuck the toe of my boot into the stirrup and grab the front of the saddle, groaning as I try to pull myself over the horse.

Which doesn't work.

I try again, flinging my leg until I'm able to climb on Leo's back. My stomach flips. I'm higher off the ground than I thought I would be. And I'm about to be *very* high off the ground.

"It's okay," I say as Leo shifts uneasily. "Just . . . go forward a little. Go."

I nudge him with my heels, and he breaks into a trot. As he speeds up to join the other horses, I'm bouncing hard in the saddle. If trotting is this hard, how in the world am I going to fly?

Honor Tumbrel sees me for the first time. His nostrils flare. I ignore him, riding ahead. Adam and his horse trot up beside me.

"Mallie Ramble," Adam says, patting his horse's silvery neck, "meet Jeff. Iggy says he's the oldest horse here and probably the slowest. But he'll get the job done." Adam swallows hard. "I hope. Did Iggy give you the lowdown?"

"No, not really."

Adam's forehead wrinkles. "Oh no. Okay . . . let's see . . . You've got to speak with authority. Hold on with your legs. Use the reins to guide the horse—gently—and nudge—don't kick—with your heel or calf. Don't yank or pull at the reins; that could hurt him . . ."

I nod quickly. "Okay, okay—nudge, don't kick. Guide, don't pull. Speak with authority."

Adam rambles on anxiously, giving me way too many directions to memorize. I feel Leo's excitement as we all ride out of the woods and begin climbing a tall green cliff. My stomach flip-flops again at the edge, but Leo isn't nervous at all. He comes to a stop at the edge of the cliff and stomps his hoof against the ground excitedly. Gravel pieces rain down into the valley far below us.

"Every horse needs to stand right on the edge," Mortimer instructs. "You won't be going far today. Just across this canyon, you'll see Mount Carson. Visibility is good today, so you shouldn't have any low Dustclouds to deal with. Just remember not to get too close to the ceiling of Dust above us, yes? You might remember Mount Carson from the rhyme you learned in school. Pinkberry trees bloom everywhere there. Pink leaves fall this time of year. But the winds around Mount Carson can be difficult to navigate. Fly to the top of Mount Carson, and you'll see gold powder clinging to the edges. Take the Keep at your side—just like you were taught—and scoop up the gold powder. It's that simple, my friends. That simple, and that hard. Steady your hearts . . . set your sights . . . go."

Suddenly, Mortimer's men shout in unison, startling the horses, startling all of us.

"Fly!" I hear the boys all shout, tapping their horses with their boot heels. So, I shout the same thing:

"Uh—fly?"

Every horse jumps—including mine.

"Whoa!" I yell. "WHOA!"

For a split second, I forget to hold on. My body reacts like I'm falling, not flying, and I drop the reins and wrap my arms around Leo's neck.

Leo soars only for a moment—then launches straight down toward the valley—so fast my face burns. He flaps his wings once, a sound so loud I nearly let go to hold my ears.

I can't remember anything Adam told me.

All I remember now is how to scream.

How am I supposed to do this? And how do I do it without throwing up?

I missed all instruction in basic riding before we launched. Now the ground is getting closer. I see the rooftops of homes in the valley. Towers and church spires and wagons so small they looked like ants a second ago.

Today's lunch swirls around way too fast in my gut.

"STOP!" I yell. But Leo curves, zooming skyward. Not sure what to do, I reach for the reins. I tug, which is not easy when flying this fast. He changes direction . . . sails back toward the cliff we just jumped from. Guardians stand on the edge now, laughing, pointing. But then they're running because they think I'll crash into them. Faster, faster, the trees on the cliff are coming toward my face. "Stop. Pull up. LEOOOO! DO SOMETHING BESIDES CRASH."

Again, Leo arches upward. I tug the reins. *Gently*, I remind myself. Just like Mama always tells me.

"Turn . . . please?"

Leo pivots his body so gracefully this time, as if he's swimming in water instead of flying through air. His left wing lowers as he swoops to the left. Mount Carson is bright pink ahead of me, and it looks like it's surrounded by a swarm of bees. But those aren't bees. They're boys on Starbirds, who are accomplishing the mission right now. I'm so far behind!

"Faster?" I ask it like a question. I don't know what to say, exactly, to communicate to Leo which way to go.

I try barely pulling the reins toward the middle, pivoting my body so I'm steering Leo with all of me and not just my arm.

I don't know if this idea is effective, because all I can see is Nico and his white horse flying right toward us.

"Mallie!" Nico shouts, waving his arm. "Move!"

"I don't know how!" I call back. But Leo does. He dives. Again.

"Stop!" I scream, tapping my heels against his side.

Leo's hooves bang down on solid ground . . . but something is wrong.

Leo has landed sideways on the cliff's face, perpendicular to the ground. The cliff we just jumped from. I hear

Mortimer's men laughing as they look over the ridge at us. Below us, the ground is rocky, and gravity is doing its best to pull me headfirst in that direction. I groan as I try to keep my upper body upright.

"Leo." I tap my heels against his side. "Off the cliff."

But Leo is busy. Eating. He's munching on the grass growing between the cracks of the rocks.

Adam said to speak with authority. I think about Mama, who is confident but still kind when she helps me work through a problem. I should try speaking like she would. With strength in my voice I command, "Leo, JUMP!" And I tap his side with my boot.

Leo's head snaps up. He lifts his front feet and pounds the cliff with his back hooves, sending a tiny waterfall of mud and dirt and rocks into the valley below.

"UP," I command firmly, and I stand in the stirrups to illustrate the point. Leo flies in a circle, like he's perfectly confused. The other horses fly past us, back toward the launch spot. They've completed the mission. Leo follows suit.

I slide farther sideways on the saddle as he zooms toward the clearing, my thigh muscles shaking as I fight to say balanced. When Leo's hooves hit the ground, I bounce off the saddle and hit the ground, too. Pain bolts up my tailbone. But the embarrassment I feel hurts even worse than the fall.

I have *nothing*. Not a drop of gold powder. Nothing in the bag on my belt. I didn't even make it to Mount Carson. What if Mortimer makes me leave now? He's seen how terrible I am. As I fight back angry tears, Leo nuzzles the side of my face. I sit up, slowly, to find Mortimer's men red-faced with laughter.

Adam lands soon after me, managing to stay on his horse. He swings off the saddle to check on me. I can see his bag is at least half-full of dirt. Honor Tumbrel lands after him, bouncing in the saddle, slowing his horse to a trot. He stares down at me, beaming.

I wipe the dust from my face and glare up at him. "Seriously? I could have fallen off my horse and bashed my skull and you think it's funny?"

"Not funny," Honor says. "Hilarious. And very satisfying."

Someone reaches to help me, and I assume it's Adam.

"I'm fine," I say, pushing the hand away. But it's the small boy I met yesterday. Greer. The new purple stripe in his spiky hair makes him look fierce. "Nobody did good out there," he says. But I know this isn't true. Every other rider got at least a little bit of gold powder. That's good. Some riders even did great.

I stand slowly so I don't fall over. I won't give them anything else to laugh at. This isn't funny to me.

"Mallie!" Mortimer calls out, concern thick in his voice. "Are you all right?"

I spin around to face him, fighting to keep the tears from my eyes. Not to mention the desperation from my voice. "I'm so sorry! Next time, I'll do better. I'll fill up four bags of gold!"

Mortimer bites his lip as he looks at my empty bag of gold powder. And then he looks in my eyes.

"I can do this," I tell him. "Another chance, and I'll give you more gold powder than any rider."

"That's a big promise to make me, Mallie," he says uncertainly.

But I shake my head. "I'm not promising it to *you*. I'm making a promise to myself. I don't break those."

He looks in my eyes a moment longer, like he's searching for something. And finally, he nods. "Of course you will. Everyone deserves a second chance." He looks at my empty bag, then back at me. "By next time, I'm sure you'll have the hang of it. I'm sure you'll do your part."

"Yes! I know I will." The sudden release of worry makes me feel tired. Exhausted, even. My disappointment in myself doesn't go away.

Greer and the rest of the boys all unhook their Keeps and hold them out. Mortimer beams, so pleased by what he sees. "We are well on our way," he says, clapping some of their shoulders as he moves around. "Iggy, make sure these boys get the Feathersworth they're owed.

"No Feathersworth for Mallie today." His hand settles on my shoulder, too. "But don't be discouraged. I have no doubt you'll complete the next mission."

Iggy shuffles up beside me and passes a small sack of Feathersworth to Greer. The clear sound of jingling coins inside reminds me of water. A whole waterfall. I stare into my empty Keep. My heart's as dry as it's ever been.

"Are you going to make fun of me, too?" I ask her.

"Nah," Iggy says with a shrug. "You're good to my horses. That's saying something."

"*Your* horses?" I ask. "What makes them your horses?"

"I've got my secrets, Mallie," Iggy says, sadness pinching her voice. "Everybody's got secrets."

15

Midnight Rider

"Mallie?"

My head, which was about to nod splat into a piece of pinkberry pie, jolts up at the sound of Mama's voice. We are all around the table together. Night has closed in around our cottage. The fire in the hearth behind us fills the room with flickering warmth and dancing shadows. An old book rests half-open on a chair arm. Blankets Mama stitched are billowed around us on the floor. The pictures Mama has drawn over the years are stuck to the walls: pictures of us when we were little; pictures of flowers, back when the sun shined. She believes the details of a place make it special. And now she's leaned in, studying the details of my face, her forehead wrinkled in worry. They've all leaned in, waiting for me to speak. Even Honeysuckle, perched on Papa's shoulder, cocks her head at me.

"I should go on to bed early," I say. "Or I'll wake up with pinkberry pie on my face."

Mama frowns. The dim light softens her features, makes her look as young as she actually is. "You hardly ate anything. How will you ride if you don't eat?"

It's the first time she's mentioned the ride since I got home. The families of the Coal Top riders were waiting when we came out of the woods tonight. Connor, Nico, and Adam all gave their families Feathersworth. The pride shined in their eyes even brighter than the coins. My family didn't come, and I was grateful, in a way. I had nothing to show for myself.

I glance down at Denver, beside me. So little his chin could rest down on the table. I swallow the lump of sadness in my throat. So much for the lucky Starpatch.

"Mama's been making you pie all day," Denver says, pushing my plate in front of me. "Eat some. And tell us what it's like to fly."

Mama scrapes a piece of pinkberry with her fork, a slash of red across her plate. "It's dangerous. We know that much."

My heart sinks again. I want my mama to be proud of me, always. I've had a long day. I really need to hear her say it now, but she doesn't. I lift a piece of pie to my mouth at the same time as I fight back tears. Mixed-up tears, from anger and hurt and flat-out fatigue. And I wonder if—for the rest of my life—I'll remember the taste of pinkberries when I get sad.

I swallow and speak: "It's a wild and wonderful feeling, too—flying. Better than any dream. Better than you could imagine."

"You're so close to the Dust," Mama says with a shiver. "You're gonna breathe all that in. Get sick and—"

"I'm careful," I say, more forcefully than I should.

Mama rises suddenly and goes to the kitchen, as if it's just another night. As if nothing strange has happened.

"I'm sorry," I say. She doesn't respond.

Papa rests a hand on my arm. He leans over to kiss the top of my head, and I fold into his hug. It's just the three of us, alone at this quiet table with an old lantern lighting the distance between us.

"I thought she'd be proud of me," I say.

Papa doesn't answer, of course. But I wish he could. Denver does: "She's proud of you. She's pie proud."

I smile at the expression on his face, so adorably thoughtful. So Denver. "Explain."

"We don't have pie stuff here anymore. Ever. That costs a bunch of Feathersworth. But today Mama went into town and bought pie stuff. Because it's a special day. Because you're our hero, and you're doing a brave thing. I think she's so worried about you that it's hard for her to say she's proud of you. Even though she means it. Mama doesn't say stuff sometimes, but she shows it. She's pie proud. I am, too."

I smile, sinking back into my seat. "You're smart for your age."

He nods. "I'm smart for any age. Now, tell me about flying."

Before I tell the story, I'm aching for some comfort. I pull off my boots and hear them drop underneath the table. The grid on the bottom of the boots is packed with yellow dust. "I stepped in Timor powder. Adam says they keep it in the mines to use as medicine sometimes? I've been seeing traces of it now that he's pointed it out. Have you heard of it?"

Denver shakes his head and I push the thought to the

back of my mind. I tell them stories about flying that make them laugh. Laugh until we yawn. Laugh until it's time for bed.

Until it's time to lock the doors. Bolt the windows. Keep the wind—and the crows—out for as long as we can.

That night, I'm asleep in seconds. But I keep jolting awake, thinking someone is there.

Trying to get in.

Breaking down the door.

Or I wake up thinking it's time to go. I used to get this way before tests in school; I would wake up all night worried I would be late.

But the room is filled with dusty darkness. My family's still sleeping. I'm the only one awake.

I imagine the sound of Leo's hooves running toward me.

The sound of him galloping—on land and on air.

The *SNAP* of his wings in the wind.

How weightless I felt for a few brief seconds in the sky, on the back of a Starbird. How much better will I feel when I bring my parents all the money we need?

I can't fail again.

I won't fail again.

THOMP.

The sound comes from the rooftop.

"What is that?" Denver asks, leaning over the bunk upside down like a wild-haired bat. "Hide me! Mallie! Go wake Mama!"

"Calm down," I whisper, rustling out of bed. I'm already at the window looking up, but I'm not worried like he is. Guardians don't come through the roof. They march right through the front door.

I glance around the side of the house. There's nothing except the trees, swaying in the wind. Then I look up again, and a big-eyed horse face looks down at me. I jump back, startled.

"What is it, Mallie?!"

"Go back to sleep," I tell Denver, tugging on one boot, then another. Why in the world would Leo come to visit me in the middle of the night?

"Why?" Denver's voice softens to a whisper. "Mallie . . . is that your horse? Is that Leo?! I want to see him!"

"You will eventually," I whisper. "But we can't wake up Mama. We don't want her to worry. Go to sleep for now. I'll be back."

I sneak outside and climb the old ladder we prop against the side of the house. It's been a long time since any of us have used the ladder—twists of ivy are spiraled over every rung now. I climb slowly, hoping none of the rungs are rotten with age. We used to climb more often. Most people use their rooftops for practical things, for drying apples and picking the ripest pinkberries that grow in the treetops. Mama said she and Papa used to let Starpatches dry up here before they wove them into book covers. Coats, quilts, and books, things that give you comfort. Things that make you dream good dreams.

Back when I was little, they'd carry me up here and point to places where the stars used to be. Where the sun used to set.

I climb gently onto the roof and see Leo, chewing loudly on some weeds growing up through the slats. He raises his head when I climb up on the top. Stops chewing.

And his mouth tips sweetly, as if he is smiling.

"You scared me," I say, leaning my face into his. "What are you doing here?"

He nuzzles my face. That's his answer. He just wants to see me.

I yawn, without realizing it. Leo kneels down on the flat rooftop and opens his wing—like he's inviting me to sit against his side. So I do. I cuddle against him, under his wing, like it's the strongest, softest blanket in the world. Because it is.

"Aren't you afraid of the monsters?" I ask. "They're always out at night. Maybe it's okay since you fly?"

Leo snorts, as if the monsters are nothing to worry about. He leans down to chomp on a piece of mint growing on the roof slats.

Ping.

An acorn bounces across the roof.

Ping.

Another, popping against Leo's nose. The horse grunts. A familiar whisper comes from down below. "Hey. Freckles."

"Adam?" I whisper as loud as I can, and crawl to the edge of the roof. Below me stands my best friend, as wide-awake as if it was true morning. He tips his hat at me. Leo clomps up beside me and looks down, too, nickering happily.

"Have you lost your mind?" I whisper-shout down below. "There are monsters in the woods at night!"

"I live just over that hill, Mallie," Adam reminds me. And then he holds up a big stick. "Plus, I'm prepared."

I groan and shake my head. There's no way a stick would keep a monster away. Even Honor Tumbrel's stupid sword won't keep the monsters away. When the Guardians are all together, they seem to be able to intimidate the monsters enough to keep them far off. But I'm no Guardian, and neither is Adam.

Leo trots across the roof to me, nickering happily.

"Shhhh," I hiss. "Stop with the walking! You'll wake Mama and Papa!"

Adam beams. "Oh, good! Leo's here! I had an idea that I came to tell you about. Now I can show you."

He puts one boot on the lowest ladder rung, and I'm waving my arms wildly.

"No! That's too many of us on the roof. I'll come down to you. Leo"—I make eye contact with my horse—"stay."

So, of course, Leo launches. He jumps off the rooftop, pops his wings open like a parachute, and sails to the ground. He's waiting for me when I get there.

"Wanna take a ride?" Adam asks, bobbing up on his toes in excitement.

"*That's* your idea?" I shake my head. "We have work tomorrow and a mission in the evening. I can't be riding tonight."

Adam shifts his weight from one foot to the other. He can't stop fidgeting tonight. It's like we're little kids again and he's convincing me to skip my chores and go play. "It's just . . ." His voice stumbles over the words. "You looked like you needed a little help today."

I narrow my eyes. "I'm doing just fine."

"I don't mean it as an insult! But you weren't even there for practice. I was. I can show you what I learned. And what I figured out on my own up there."

"How are we going to ride if your horse isn't here?"

"We can both ride Leo."

"Ride him . . . together?"

"Sure. I brought a rope; I was going to show you my plan on that fallen tree over there. But we can make it into a halter and reins for Leo." Adam works quickly. Then he gives me a boost, and I sling my leg over Leo's back.

"What you have to learn to do," Adam says, "is guide him with your body. Lean forward to go. Lean back to stop. Maybe you could just keep the reins in your left hand—don't worry about hooking the right arm through. Lift to the left or right from the center—but don't pull too hard."

I raise an eyebrow. Sure, I feel connected to Leo. But I feel off balance on his back, and trying to guide him with my body—when my body feels so shaky—doesn't make sense. Still, I try pulling the reins toward the middle with my left hand, pivoting my body so I can steer Leo with all of me and not just my arms.

"And when you need to grab gold powder," Adam says, "you can loop your right arm through the slack, just above your Popsnap. It'll take a little practice, maybe. But Iggy says it takes practice for everybody."

"She hates me," I mumble. I let the reins slide through my left hand until I'm holding on in the middle. Lean forward to go. Lean back to stop. Tug left. Tug right.

"I think she's just . . . matter-of-fact. And I think we'll like her a lot once we get to know her."

It's a valid point, as much as I hate to admit it. I think it's easy to pretend you know all about a person when you've met them once. And who knows what was going on in that person's heart and mind when you had that first chance meeting.

"Iggy's smart about horses," Adam says. "She said the trick is you hold on with your legs. Steer with your body. And with your voice. She says to speak with authority, but that doesn't mean shouting."

He gently taps Leo's side. My horse trots through the dark woods, and his footsteps are all I hear. Mama keeps a lantern burning all night in our cottage. It's a tiny flicker and barely illuminates anything out here.

"First of all," I say quietly, "how does Iggy know how to ride a Starbird? I bet we know as much as she does. Second, I tried all of that and it didn't help!"

"Not really. You told Leo what to do like you were asking him a question."

"I was doing better at the end. I think I almost had the hang of it, but I didn't have enough time." My shoulders slump. "My confidence is pretty shot after today."

"Everybody had a hard time on their horses today."

"You didn't! You got a thousand Feathersworth!"

"I barely got enough gold powder to fill that sack," Adam says. "You just couldn't tell because you were focused on your own ride. Some of those horses were trying to buck guys off."

My heart warms at this. "Even Honor?"

He chuckles. "Honor was being bucked all over the sky. He managed to scrape some gold powder, but he looked as silly as everybody else doing it."

I sigh happily. "Music to my ears."

"Tell Leo to go straight," Adam says.

As Leo trots ahead, the cottage light gets farther away. I can't see my arms, my horse. I can't see what's ahead of us or around us. I feel invisible, like a shadow. I wonder if this is how mountain people felt when the stars went away, when the light was snuffed out. I turn my head to look back at the lantern light—so small, barely visible. It's a pinprick. A firefly. But it is light. The dark can never take it all away. "We shouldn't go too far," I tell Adam. "The monsters—"

"Leo will get us out of here if monsters come," Adam says. "I have a feeling a horse could stomp down a monster any day."

I remember back to the night I met Leo in the woods. "I think so, too."

"So," Adam says after a time, "want to try flying again?"

A hard knot of anxiety settles in my stomach. "Now? We're not supposed to be out at night."

"Who's going to know?"

"Somebody will see," I say. "And even if the monsters are afraid of horses, they might still attack me and you."

"There are no monsters in the sky," he says. "Don't you want to learn how to do this? So when we ride again, you can actually get paid?"

"I'll kill us both, probably," I say.

"Probably."

Adam laughs a little, and it's warm on my neck. He wraps his arms around my waist. And that feeling of anxiety—plus something else, a whole new kind of nervous—climbs up into my throat. Steals my voice away. I don't think Adam's been this close to me before. Ever.

And I don't think I mind.

I nudge Leo's sides gently with my heels, and we trot into the dark woods.

As much as I hate to admit it, Iggy is right: If I hold on tight with my legs, I don't feel all shook up. My whole body doesn't rattle anymore; I'm right in stride with Leo.

"Want to try it in the air?" Adam says after a while.

"Yes!"

"All right, so Iggy says horses need a good run to take off," Adam says, an edge of excitement in his voice. "They accelerate faster. Earlier, they basically just launched off the cliffs—which is okay. But they launch easier with a run."

"Leo." I say his name with authority. Gentle authority. I change my posture, shoulders back, legs tight, eyes straight ahead. I lean forward, smile, and say: "RUN." Leo gallops into the woods, hooves slamming against the ground. The distance stretches out greater between each stride.

Leo,

    leaping.

       Trees,

          blurring.

Wind,

a western wind,

warm in the cold night,

*and full on our faces as
Leo jumps . . .*

and he never hits the ground.

He soars, up and up.

Stomach swirling.

Breath catching.

I lean forward, keeping my legs tight against Leo's sides, like Adam said to do. "Steady on," I say. "Steady on toward the sky." His flight is smooth, solid. Adam lifts his arms and shouts, "Woo-hooo!" into the night.

"Try to steer him left," Adam yells over the wind. "Just lift the reins—gently—to the left."

Gently, just like Mama said. *She'd probably be a natural with Starbirds,* I think.

I lift the reins and speak to Leo at the same time. And he swoops to the left in a motion so fluid that I barely feel it.

I shriek with happiness. And then . . . I'm the one laughing. "Leo did it!"

"You did it, Freckles! You and Leo."

"You did it," I tell him sincerely. "You taught me how."

I hear a smile in his voice when he says: "We're a good team, I guess."

"It's a fact," I agree. "I would fly anywhere with you."

And I mean that. I really would. It's easy to stand beside someone when the world is safe, when you're both sure-footed on solid ground. But I believe there are only a handful of people who make you feel like you could ride out a storm cloud. Face the darkest night. Battle a monster. Withstand the Dust. Survive anything. Make you feel brave and wanted, simply because they're right there with you.

I curve Leo toward the river. I see his shadow on the water—my beautiful night bird, backlit by the lantern lights hung on tall posts along the shore. His shadow stretches over the water. He sails so low that the tips of his hooves trace the surface, sending a silver slash across the sea.

"UP!" I yell. And we're skyward again, sailing over the pine trees, circling the North Woods.

With every turn, I feel stronger on Leo's back. I adjust easy now when he moves, hold tight with my legs as he flies. Now I'm ready for the next mission. And not just ready, I'm excited. I want them to see what I can do. Soon, I'll walk into our bright little cottage and give my parents the thousand Feathersworth that I earned. Worry will lift from their shoulders, as easy as fog lifting from the mountains. I'll be their hero.

I know I have to get home. But I don't want this night to end. "Land him easy, Mallie," Adam reminds me. We're still above the treetops—fifty feet at least. Looking down makes my stomach swirl a little, but then I remember what I've learned.

"Easy, Leo . . ." I say. "Go down." Leo's moving too fast toward the ground. Treetops are closer, sharper. I imagine hitting them at this speed. The ground that was miles below me seems to be spreading, speeding toward our faces. "Easy!" I shout.

"Oh!" Adam says, reaching around me to tug on the reins. "Sit back and say land! SITBACKANDSAYLAND!"

But he says it at the same time that Leo slams down onto the forest floor. Adam and I both bounce off his back and thump onto the ground. A little bruised, but otherwise fine, we lie in the damp leaves laughing. Leo helps himself to a spray of eucalyptus leaves dangling from a tree.

Adam's laugh—I've missed that so much. His laugh is a guffaw that always makes me laugh, too.

"We'll work on landings some other time," he says, standing up. He reaches for me—one hand holding mine—the other gently bracing my right elbow.

"Thank you," I say, dusting off my pajamas. "For everything, thank you. See you tomorrow? At the mission?"

Adam nods, tips his hat, and meanders away into the woods, down toward his house over the hill. Swinging his stupid monster stick.

"Walk him home?" I whisper to Leo. "Make sure he gets there safe?" I kiss my horse's soft muzzle. Leo trots off as sweetly as an old dog, wings pinned to his sides.

"Hey, Freckles," Adam calls when he's up ahead in the darkness, so far gone in the trees that I can't see him anymore. "I'd fly anywhere with you, too."

My heart—which I sometimes think is as Dust-covered as everything else on this mountain—shivers like a Starpatch.

16

The Pember Range

The next afternoon, Honor Tumbrel has sword practice, so nothing stops me from dashing out of the Tumbrel house as soon as my chores are done. Honeysuckle chirps short little bursts in my ear, cheering me onward to the mission ahead. There's less than a week left before the Guardians come back and no Feathersworth to show for it. All of that changes today.

Down in the valley, nobody's talking about the horses. But when I get off the train at the mountain, there's an excited buzz all along the platform like I've never heard before.

People tip their hats to me as I pass by.

A little girl runs up to me and gives me a bloom from a pinkberry tree. When I reach out to take it, I see that she's chalked a green stripe in her hair—just like mine.

Maybe my own mama's not proud. But other people are. There's a quiet kind of hope stirring on the mountain now. I tuck the flower in my hair and decide: This time, I'm not just going to fill my Keep. I'm going to overflow it. I'll collect more gold powder for Mr. Good than he's ever dreamed.

I have to. Every time I see boys limp off the train and toward home—their heads bowed, eyes inky-black, I know: I have to.

Adam and Greer are waiting for me at the end of the platform. And so is Ms. Marcia. She's chatting with the boys, holding a big, steaming crate in her arms. I can tell by the cinnamon smell—and the smile on the boys' faces—exactly what it is. Apple puffs—a giant, steaming crateful of apple puffs. Normally, I would be excited, too. Today, I have no time to stop and make small talk. I have to get to the clearing.

"Hold on a second, Mallie!" Ms. Marcia calls out. She's one of the brightest things on this dusty mountain, besides Granny Mab and the Dustflights. She makes clothes out of old curtains the valley people throw out, clothes that look better than anything *they* wear. She stains her lips with pinkberries and has a parasol made of quilt scraps. It's not like there's any sunlight she needs to shield her face from. She just misses color, she says.

"I wish I could talk, Ms. Marcia," I tell her. "But I—"

"I made apple puffs for all of you sweet kids riding today," she says, carrying on like I've said nothing. "And for your horses, too. Everything in here is safe for a horse to eat."

"That's so kind of you. But I have to—"

"Relax, Mallie," Adam says, shoving a puff in his mouth. "We have plenty of time."

Ms. Marcia leans down and whispers, "I used to ride Starbirds when I was a girl."

Granny Mab rolls her cart up beside us, chewing a long green pipe. "So did I! But my mother wouldn't let me fly."

"Neither did mine," Ms. Marcia says, "but I did anyway. I hope they stay. I hope they're back to stay. There's talk, you know. Talk in town about how, if the Starbirds are back . . . maybe the stars will be back someday, too.

That'd be something, wouldn't it? If the stars shined again in our lifetime?"

I nod. "It would."

Ms. Marcia gives me a steaming apple puff, wrapped in waxy brown paper. "Eat this and remember better days," she says. Starpatches used to be particularly clingy in apple trees, and some people believe you still get a little bit of starlight inside you when you eat them. You still feel happy like people did back then. I don't know if that's true. I just think taste has a memory sometimes—and our memory of starlight is a fine feast.

"I have something for you, too, Mallie," Granny Mab says, fishing through the goods in her cart. She passes me a package wrapped in old newspaper.

"I don't have money to buy anything . . ."

Granny Mab waves the notion away. "Consider it a gift."

I tear the package open and unfold a pair of gray long-sleeved coveralls. They're exactly my size.

"That'll make it much easier to ride!" Granny Mab says. "Ms. Marcia painted the wording on the back."

Green swirling letters—the same green as the stripe in my hair—spell out *Mallie over the Moon* from shoulder to shoulder. Bright silver stitches seam the sides. I touch the thread and my heart jolts.

"I saved that thread for something special," Ms. Marcia says. She and Granny Mab are both smiling big, eyes alight with the joy that comes when you know you've given someone the perfect gift.

And I do mean *perfect*.

"This," I tell her sincerely, "is wonderwow."

"Go try it on, then," Granny Mab says, shooing me off into the woods. "Hurry. You have a mission to get to."

When I come back, Granny Mab and Ms. Marcia are applauding in delight. Greer is smiling, and Adam is . . . staring

"Does it look . . . weird?" I ask him.

He swallows visibly and shakes his head. "Not weird. Not even a little bit. You'll look like the toughest rider in the sky."

Mab pulls a cracked mirror from her cart and spins me around—thankfully—before Adam sees how red my face is. She holds up the mirror so I can see myself.

Pretty. It's such a weird word because it means so many things. I've heard some girls say they felt pretty—beautiful, even—when they look at themselves in a fluffy dress. That used to be a tradition in Coal Top—ordering dresses for our fourteenth birthdays, made in our favorite colors, decked out with charms of our favorite flowers. But that ended when the Dust came. There was no time for frivolous fun anymore.

And really, I didn't mind that I would never experience it. I've never felt great in a dress—just awkward and itchy.

But I feel beautiful in this. It's just gray—gray as the sky and the Dust in the mines. But it does look tough on me. Strong. Strong like the Dust smudged on my face. The green stripe shining in my hair, bright as spring trees after the rains. I don't cuff the sleeves, like I've seen other boys do when they ride, because I don't want my Popsnap to be obvious.

Before I realize what I'm even doing, I twirl.

Ms. Marcia giggles, and Granny Mab chuckles.

"Now you look ready to ride," Granny Mab says. "Now you look like Mallie over the Moon."

We do get to the clearing in plenty of time, so Adam and I distribute apple puffs to the rest of the boys getting ready to ride. I even offer one to Honor, because my silver-stitched coveralls are making me so darn happy. But he rolls his eyes.

"Nice outfit," he says with a smirk. "Looks like the clothes boys are given when they go work in the mines. Wonder if Denver will have a matching one soon?"

I clutch an apple puff in my hand and prepare to throw it directly at the center of his giant forehead, when Greer grabs my hand and pulls me away.

"Aw'right, now!" Iggy marches up on the stage. "Pay attention, you daisy-brained knuckleheads. Quit jabbering."

Her hair is tucked up into the brown knit hat again, and she's looking at her endless checklist. "Listen up, 'cause I'm only saying all this once! Today, you'll be snatching gold from the Pember Mountains. MAP!"

The mighty Pembers, our snowy giants. These have always been my favorite mountains to see. The best time to spot them is in winter, on a morning ride down the mountain. Their white peaks always make me think of a castle, a kingdom, somewhere far away. Barely visible through a haze of gray Dust. They made me believe fairy tales exist somewhere.

Now I'll get to see them up close.

The Guardians unravel the map from the trees at Iggy's command, reminding us how far the Pember Mountains actually are from where we stand.

Iggy continues: "So, you leave these woods and fly north. See? And you head for the mountain range all covered in snow. It'll take you an hour, tops. Maybe two, if you've got a slow horse." She smiles at Adam's horse, Jeff. Adam pets Jeff's muzzle.

"Seems easy enough, right?" Iggy asks. And then she shouts: "Well, it's not! It's freezing cold, to start with. So there's hats and scarves up here, and you better wear them. You'll freeze to death if you don't. There's also special goggles, sent by Mr. Good—those'll help you see even when the blizzard's howling at you. Which it will be. Mr. Good'll be here when you return to weigh the gold powder and distribute your Feathersworth. *If* you earn them. So good luck and try not to die, 'kay? And be careful with my horses!"

And with that, she's done.

"Let's ride," I say, nodding to Adam and Greer.

We hook the Keeps to our belts. This is the one thing I haven't practiced, reaching down to unhook my Keep and collect gold powder. But I feel better about riding at least. We pull on hats, knitted scarves, and round goggles. And then I feel something—someone—tap my leg.

"Need any more tips, Mallie?" Iggy is standing in front of me, tiny hands propped on her hips. "Or you going to put on another show today?"

"No, I'm going to ride today. And by the way, it's easy to stand down here and tell people what to do. It's harder to get up there and actually do it."

Her lips curl into a grimace. "You don't know a thing about me, Mallie-brains. Everybody's—"

"Got secrets," I finish for her. "Whatever. My name is Mallie. Not Mallie-brains. Not Mallie in the Muck. Just Mallie. Of all people, you shouldn't be making fun of my name." I cock my head at her, curious. "Is Iggy even your real name?"

"It's none of your business, but yes! Iggy's my given name! Iggy Thump is what my dad called me. I've been called all sorts of other things. Mostly on account of my height. Shorty, mostly. Half-pint. Gnome girl. People always describe my height first. Happens when you're small. Tall, too, probably. I've also been called loud-mouthed and temper-prone and boyish. Boyish! Like that's a bad thing. It's a pet peeve of mine, when people say *girlish* or *boyish* like it's an actual insult. Doesn't bother me. Because I'm proud of who I am. I *know* who I am."

"I really wasn't trying to make you mad," I assure her. I didn't realize Iggy would launch into a rant. "I was honestly just curious."

"I'm not finished!" Iggy jabs her finger at her chest, like she's pointing to her heart. "The name my papa gave me was Iggy Thump. He also called me brave and smart and wonderful. So, Iggy means all that to me. So you can call me crabby if you want, Mallie-girl. You might be crabby, too, if you were missing somebody like I am. I don't care what you call me. Because love told me who I am. That's all I have to say to you."

And she stomps away, her little boots making faint impressions through the dusty mud.

Leo gives me a side-eyed glance.

"I'm sorry," I tell him. "I was just asking! I'll apologize when we get back."

"Mount up!" Iggy hollers from the center of the clearing. "You don't have all night!"

I can tell the boys are already getting more confident as riders. They gallop, side by side, laughing, trying to shove each other off their horses, and howl delightedly as they soar into the sky. I wait for all the riders to go. I watch them all fly off, headed into the dusty horizon. Maybe it's just a game to them. But this is so much more to me. Four rides and we're out of debt. A few more than that . . . and maybe I can build a whole new life.

"Ready?" Adam says, riding up beside me. I nod and mount Leo.

In the saddle, I take the reins in my hand.

Riders are mounting up on every side of me. The horses are shaking their heads and flicking their ears in excitement.

A signal from one of the Guardians, and we gently lead the horses into a trot.

Mountain girl, lift up your eyes,
The stars are shining bright for thee.

I don't sing the words this time, but I feel them—let them roll through me as the horses begin to gallop. I am a mountain girl. I am born to fly. And this flight will change everything.

The sound of horse hooves pounding the ground echoes like thunder through my chest. Ahead of me, I see a few horses jumping into flight: Honor Tumbrel, then his friends, then Greer and the boys from Coal Top.

Steady. Out of the corner of my eye, I see Iggy watching everyone fly away. Her arms are wrapped tight around her tiny chest, as if she's trying to give herself a hug.

Leo is leaping already. Aching to be airborne. I'm aching, too. I keep him steady for a while longer, but I can already feel the sky calling to me, pulling me up into its wind. Riders are already far ahead of us in the sky, disappearing specks in the haze.

I tap my heels against Leo's sides.

Once.

Twice.

"Leo, fly."

Leo launches into the air.

"Good boy," I say as my breath whooshes out of me again. "We can do this . . ."

I want to remember every second of this ascent later, to tell Denver. He'll ask me. He'll want to know what it's like. But how do you describe something this magical?

As Leo rises, my stomach feels hollow. I'm light as air up here. I feel boundless. Soon enough, a feeling like fear flutters inside that hollow place. But the higher we climb, the more it mellows into joy. I couldn't wipe this smile off my face even if I wanted to.

The Dust is far enough above me that it's not affecting me, and I imagine being able to fly above it. To leave a hole in the darkness.

Leo's hooves beat against the wind; he's running on air. And we're soaring.

"Look down there!" Adam yells as he flies up beside me. "There's Coal Top!"

I hadn't imagined seeing my home from up above. Yesterday, I was too busy trying not to fall off and die to notice anything else. But now I see it all clearly. So many little cottages. Little windows like fiery animal eyes in the woods. *So much love and worry under those rooftops*, I realize. We pass over the North Woods, right over my house. I can't see it through the trees, but it's down there. I know it. Maybe Mama sees me, too. Maybe she's telling Papa about it right now, about how brave I look up here. And then, like that, Coal Top is behind me. A place that holds my entire life story so far can be seen in a blink from up above.

We fly for miles, and the wind gets cool, then colder. I see riders to my left and right. Horses soaring steadily, occasionally flapping their wings.

"Watch for low-flung Dust!" Adam yells. The Dust is a good hundred feet above us, but small cloudy patches loom low. They're Dustblobs in the sky, basically. Leo and I swirl around them with ease. All the riders curve right to avoid a huge Dustcloud . . . and that's when we see the mountain: jagged and snow-covered.

Icy, sharp, tall enough to nearly touch the Dust: The Pember Range is waiting.

The air turned snow-freckled at first, but now the snow looks like feathers. Falling around us, thickening as we get closer, shooting as fast as a thousand white stars as we fly upward. My face burns against the cold.

"Steady!" I tell Leo, leaning forward just slightly. He sails into position easily, toward the first jagged peak.

A howl of wind pushes against us, blowing us all into one another's paths. Greer crashes into my side. "Sorry, Mallie!"

The jolt nearly knocks the reins from my hand, but

I right myself. I feel Leo's body trembling as he fights to stay straight.

I double-check my goggles, making sure they're tight against my face, and flip a notch just above the lens. Not only does this help me see through the blinding snow, but it helps me see details, too. Shiny details. The mountaintop, in particular, is absolutely sparkling. That's the gold powder we're after. Riders are already swooping toward it, but snatching no more than a handful of dust before the wind blows them off course.

I come up with a better idea.

I lean into Leo, resting my face against his mane. "DOWN!"

Leo nosedives, his wings pinned hard against my legs. When we're halfway down the mountain, I tug the reins gently and give two commands: "Land, Leo! Climb!"

His wings expand wide open.

Hooves crash against the mountainside as he lands, vertically. Rocks and ice shatter toward the ground as he races up the side of one of the Pember Mountains. I lean my body weight forward, holding tight to the reins. Beside me, Adam does the same.

I grit my teeth against the pull of gravity. Against the cold wind on my cheeks.

When I see a sparkle in my goggles, I unhook my Keep,

lean low, and swoop it along the mountain edge. The bag is heavy when I pull it back up! My heart soars when I glance at the bag and see that the inside is sparkling.

We summit, and I shout, "Leo! Jump!"

Adam and I both holler for joy as Leo and Jeff jump from the peak, diving toward the other side of the mountain.

Again, Leo lands at a vertical gallop on the mountain-side. Now other riders have watched us, and they're doing the same thing. I stand in the stirrups, fighting gravity not to fall off the back of my horse as he races to the top.

Gold powder,

     snatched.

         Wind,

              howling.

                   "Leo. Jump!"

My bag's nearly full!

Leo neighs wildly as he soars through the air. His wings open wide, sailing, and I know he needs a quick rest before we dive and scale the next hill. I look to my side, to tell Adam.

Thump! Something slams against my shoulder, and my vision blurs. Pain zings across my back. I look up and realize Adam is gone. Honor Tremble is flying beside me now.

He settles his boot back in the stirrup and smirks.

"What are you *doing*?" I shout.

He answers by standing tall in the saddle and kicking at me. *Again.*

"No!" I shout as I stand in the stirrups and lean forward. "Go, Leo!"

Leo pulls away, just missing the heel of Honor's boot.

"Stop that!" I yell behind me.

In one solid move, Honor pulls his sword loose and punches a hole in my Keep. "No!" I shout, grabbing it in my hand as gold powder falls through my fingers.

"Mallie!" Greer flies overhead, then swoops down beside me, holding out a piece of chewed gum. "I know it's gross, but—"

"It's great!" I say, working quickly to patch the gum against the hole.

I see Honor zooming ahead of me, and I reattach my Keep to my belt.

"Go," I command, through clenched teeth, pulling against the reins to steer Leo toward that one impossibly tall, jagged summit ahead of us. I won't let anything stop me this time: not Honor, not the weather, not the howling wind. I *will* fill my Keep.

The snow falls in spirals.

Ice crystalizes against my face,

my hand,

my horse's hair.

But Leo doesn't stop. And neither will I.

"Dive!"

I grit my teeth. Tighten my legs against Leo's sides.

Diving

> *down,*

>> *down,*

>>> *down and . . .*

At the last possible second, I gently tug the reins, and Leo's hooves slam into the mountain. We gallop to the top, racing Honor Tremble, both filling our sacks with gold powder.

I won't let him intimidate me.

I'm not Mallie in the Muck today.

I'm Mallie over the Moon.

I wish Mama could see.

I wish Papa could be here . . .

I think these things—and a thousand others—as I scrape gold powder off the surface of the icy mountain. We *did* it.

As Leo jumps from the summit, I realize we are basically at the world's ceiling. I see Forgotten Mountain far, far away from me. And the Dust . . . I can almost touch it. I want to. I never imagined I would be this close.

I lift my left arm, stretching my fingertips, longing for the grit of it on my skin. "Climb, Leo," I whisper. "Just a little higher . . ."

Here's the weird thing: The closer I get, the angrier I feel. Not just angry—but I feel rage. I imagine breaking Honor's nose, stomping his shoulder like he did mine. Hurting things. Breaking things. There's a scream inside me, deep, trying to get loose.

"Higher," I bark.

But Leo sails low, with a sad whinny.

As we get farther from the Dust, my anger fades to sheer fatigue, and I collapse against Leo's back.

Be gentle, Mallie, I hear Mama whisper as Leo flies me toward home.

Over Windy Valley.

Forgotten Mountain rising high above it.

As we fly in a lazy circle, I see lights from lanterns on

front porches piercing the night. Little bonfires here and there. And I am so proud of the place I come from. Maybe we lost the starlight years ago. But I wonder if people there know how much they still shine from far away.

Dusk has settled over the clearing by the time everyone returns. Lanterns flicker around our camp, and riders are circled around tiny bonfires for a rest. Mortimer and his men weigh our gold powder. Leo and the other horses have gone with Iggy for a rest. I stand beside the boys from Coal Top, waiting for my reward.

"A thousand Feathersworth for Mallie Ramble," Mortimer says, dropping the sack into my shaking hand. "And we'll make sure you have a new Keep before next ride." And just like that my fatigue is eclipsed by a rush of wild joy. I'm closer than I've ever been to paying off our debt—with just one ride! He might as well have just given me the world.

Mortimer smiles his enchanting smile. "Well done, Ms. Ramble."

And then he walks to the center of where we stand and holds up his arms, to make a decree.

"As you know, these woods are not safe at night. And since you put your lives in danger while you fly, I don't think it's . . . *right* of us to ask you to put your lives in danger going home. You'll camp here tonight. The Guardians and I will watch over you."

"My parents will be so worried!" I say, stepping forward. My thoughts are immediately echoed by other boys in the clearing. All our families are struggling. They all depend on us.

"I understand," Mortimer says gently. "I will send word to your families that you're safe."

I glance down so my eyes don't betray the sudden dread I feel. How will he send word? A Guardian? Will they find Denver? I remind myself that Denver is hidden. Mama is watching the woods closely.

"Granny Mab is watching the woods, too," Adam whispers beside me, as if he can hear the thoughts swirling through my mind. "He's hidden, Mallie. He'll be okay."

One of the Guardians runs up to Mortimer and whispers in his ear.

The bonfire flickers against his face as the smile fades, and a change comes over his eyes. They look cold now, void of the spark we've become so used to. I feel myself cowering away from the look on his face.

"Moments ago," Mortimer begins, with an edge in his voice, "we had nearly twenty pounds of gold powder. Now the scales are showing we have around fifteen pounds. These are hard times, friends. But stealing won't be tolerated on these missions. I'll give the thief half an hour to return the gold—quietly. If it's not returned, rest assured that I will find out who you are." His eyes bore into ours as he looks around the clearing. He rests his hand on his sword. "And you'll no longer be a rider."

One of the Guardians strides up beside Mortimer. He's young and tall, and he keeps his hand on his sword hilt all the time—the same as Honor does. "I'd watch myself, if I were you," he tells us. "Dark hearts call out to the monsters. Thieves and liars will bring them around faster than anything. Watch and see."

Mortimer stomps away with the Guardians to a tall tent they've set up in the far corner of the clearing. Whispers rise all around the camp. I look at Adam and Greer. "We've got to watch each other's stuff. You know Honor and his friends are going to try to pin this on us."

They nod their heads, and we pull our packs close to us. I won't go to sleep. I'll watch all night if I have to. Darkness creeps in around us, and sometimes I think I can feel Honor's eyes on me in the dark. Someone's eyes, at least.

As the night settles in, the air feels dusky. We wrap our scarves around our noses and huddle close to one another, telling stories. And I that's when I feel him—my horse.

I look and see Leo standing back in the trees, watching me. The firelights in the clearing shine faintly on his coat.

"He wants me to go to him," I whisper.

Adam turns to look. "You can't. The monsters . . ."

"He protected me from the monsters once," I say. "There's something he wants to show me."

I push my pack toward him. "Keep an eye on that for me?"

He nods, taking the pack under his other arm. And I slink away into the woods to my horse.

"What's wrong?" I ask, reaching up to touch Leo's sweet face.

He walks, slowly enough for me to keep in stride easily. For an animal so big, Leo can be so quiet. No twigs pop under his hooves. There's no rustling in the forest as we get farther from the clearing. As the light drifts farther away from us, I lean in closer to Leo. Just because he saved me once from a monster, does that mean he can save me again? What if this one sneaks up on both of us? What if something is watching us right now?

Leo pauses, and so do I. There is light ahead, so I wait, giving my eyes enough time to adjust to the darkness, to this new fire we've discovered. What would anybody be doing this far from camp?

The light is the fire of a large lantern burning up ahead of us, down in the woods just to the right. Mortimer and a few of the Guardians are gathered around the flame. They're standing in a circle, whispering things to one another. I watch as Mortimer kneels down to the ground and sprinkles something in the dirt. He stirs circles, mixing it with the dark soil below. Then he presses his fingers together and makes a pulling motion. The process repeats, stir and *pull*, stir and *pull*. The Guardians all take a step back, their eyes focused on Mortimer's work. One of them rests a hand on his sword as he watches, ready to strike whenever necessary.

The Dust below Mortimer's hand begins to rise from the ground, slipping through his fingers. The push and pull reminds me of Mama kneading bread dough.

As Mortimer works, the Dust underneath his hands begins to billow. Even from here, I see what looks like a tail on one end, swishing. A pointed snout on the other. Mortimer's eyes are closed, he's muttering something, and the creature's back goes rigid instead of smooth, scales prickling all across its spine.

Did he just create that? I wonder. But that doesn't make sense. The Guardians *protect* us from creatures like this. Maybe Mortimer's just cornered something, and my eyes are playing tricks on me.

So why does it look like that thing is growing as Mortimer molds it?

I realize now my body is shaking uncontrollably. Leo is steady against my side, leaning in to support me.

They're just catching it, I tell myself.

A Guardian steps to the side, and the creature—this snake—begins to move away from their circle. I only see patches of its body in the firelight, the way its scales shine as it slithers through the forest. Mortimer and his Guardians wait for a moment, quietly. Then they follow close behind as the snake monster heads into the woods.

I have to warn everyone at the camp. Energy launches me off the ground and onto Leo. I ride him bareback through the woods, branches swatting at my face, but I don't care. I have to warn Adam and the rest of the riders that this creature is heading toward them.

"Faster," I urge. I'm back at the tree line, the campground in front of me, when I hear a scream and realize I'm too late.

A glimmer of light catches my eye, coming from across the way. The snake shimmers, slithers, through the brush and toward the camp.

"Run!" I shout, riding out of the trees on Leo's back. "RUN!"

Boys are glancing around frantically. I point to a sight that's haunted my nightmares for months, a vision so similar to what I saw the night I met Leo: bright yellow eyes. Dark slits down the center.

At the sight of the snake, Adam howls. "GO!" he yells to Greer, grabbing the little boy by the sleeve and pulling him to his feet. Nico and Connor grab our bags and run, and everyone else follows suit. But in this darkness—with all this Dust kicked up—we can't see the Dustsnake anymore.

Honor and his friends are still settled around the campfire, looking bored.

"It's a monster!" I yell. He shakes his head as if he doesn't believe me, and then one of his friends points, screams, and pulls Honor to his feet. They all push Honor in front of their group.

"You're the one with the sword!" one says. "Kill it!"

"Kill what? I can't even see it!" Honor screams. He holds the sword straight out in front of him, blade trembling so hard it dances with the bonfire light.

I squint into the night and see the monster gliding around in the chaos, as if it's enjoying it all. Shining eyes. Fangs like fire. Honor screams, shoves away from his friends, and runs.

As the monster glides past us, Leo bangs his hooves down into the clearing, barely missing the head. I slide down from his back, grab a flaming stick from one of the bonfires and hold it out in front of me. I see other boys do the same, trying something, anything, to ward off this thing.

"Where are the Guardians?" Adam shouts. "They're supposed to protect us!"

I look all around and see no one. Did Mortimer lose sight of the monster in the woods? Don't they realize it's come into the clearing?

I hear ragged breathing beside me and see Honor holding his stupid sword.

"Kill it," I tell him. "Or give me the sword and I'll kill it."

The monster flings its body toward us and Honor hacks at it, madly, cutting long slashes in the dirt.

"Wait! Everybody be still!" one of Honor's friends shouts. He's holding a paper sack out in front of him, far away as if it's poisoned. As if he wants nothing to do with it. "That Guardian said the monsters know liars." A tear wriggles down the boy's face. I see the glimmer in the firelight. "Maybe if I confess, it will leave us alone."

The boy steps toward a bonfire at the center of the clearing. And slowly, in a ripple of fiery scales, the monster raises its head, yellow eyes fixed on the boy.

"I'm sorry," the boy says. He tosses the sack on the ground, and the stolen gold powder spills out.

With a wild scream, just like we heard in the woods, the snake leaps at the boy. He jumps away just in time and the snake lands in the fire, where it explodes in a tiny pouf of sparkly dirt.

The clearing grows quiet. We stand, watching, with our torches and tired eyes.

One of the Guardians walks over and takes the sack of gold from the crying boy. All the Guardians are back now, watching us from the edge of the clearing. They say nothing. They don't comfort us. Even Mortimer just watches, arms crossed over his chest.

Adam walks up beside me. "Did you see where it came from?"

For reasons I don't understand, I answer: "No."

It's only a small lie, the size of a seed. I don't like how it feels planted deep inside me.

It's still dark when I run home the next morning. Mama must be terrified, I know. I'm surprised she didn't run through the woods to find me. Even though Mortimer sent word.

Did he send a Guardian to my house?

Worry is a waterfall, drawing out every other thought in my mind.

Are the North Woods always this quiet?

I'm rounding the rough path to the cottage when I see Granny Mab up ahead. She's standing against a tree, well hidden in the dim light, black skirt billowing. She holds a finger to her lips. *Shhhh.*

Through the trees, I see the lantern lights on the front of our cottage. And there on the steps, I see billowing black cloaks. The Guardians.

Mab points up, into an old Telling Tree. The Telling Trees "tell" us the weather, usually. They turn white in the rain. They're pitch on an ordinary morning, like this one. Black as a shadow. My eyes adjust to see Denver curled up in one of the high branches, perfectly hidden.

Gentle, I remind my heart. *Stay gentle. For Denver, for now, stay silent.*

"When, exactly, will your son be home?" The Guardian is questioning Mama. "Time's running short, and so is our patience."

I clench the Feathersworth in my hand. I remember flying, just last night, with Leo. Sailing into the snow. Every day I'm getting closer. I will beat these horrible men.

I wait until they're long gone to climb into the tree. Until Honeysuckle sings out soft and low and lets us know we can be at peace. For now. She flaps up beside me as I climb. I take Denver into my arms and think about the day I taught him to climb this tree. I never realized I was teaching him to hide.

"You're not even shaking," I whisper. "Look at you, how brave you are."

"Because I saw you yesterday," he says, his voice barely a breath. "I saw you on Leo. I saw you fly. And I knew I would be all right."

For now, for this one quiet moment, he is.

17

Truth and Flame

"Hurry your butts, Coal Tops," Iggy shouts as we arrive in the clearing. "Long flight today. Let's saddle the horses and send you off."

I barely slept last night thinking about this challenge. I only need to complete three more rides and our debts are paid.

"Do you know where we're going today?" I ask. Leo

boops his nose against my forehead, and I laugh for the first time in days.

"I do," Iggy says, feeding Leo handfuls of hay. "You'll know it, too. The mountain called Truth and Flame."

"Oh!" Adam is trying to pull Jeff toward us. But Jeff is content to munch on every spare blade of grass he finds today. Adam clears his throat and says:

> From far away,
> This mountain fine,
> Looks made for walks and hikes and climbs.
> But woe to him who only sees
> Above the ground,
> And not beneath.
> No man's rank or build or family name
> Will be remembered on Truth or Flame.

"Is it just like the rhyme says?" I ask Iggy, excitement bubbling inside me. "Nice on the outside and . . . ?"

"A bold and blazing inferno on the inside." Iggy nods. "Truth and Flame would be a simple enough ride if it weren't for the blazes themselves—unexpected, hissing, bursting from pockets in the mountainside. Horses can sense the flame, of course. But it makes fetching gold hard.

So trust your ride today. I don't want the horses hurt. I'll hold you responsible if they are."

"I know," I tell her. And I agree with her, totally. It is my job to take care of Leo. Just like he takes care of me. The last conversation I had with Iggy plays through my mind. I know I should apologize, but I turn to wander away. Leo moves in front of me, blocking my path of escape, and nudges me back toward her.

"Fine," I whisper. "Iggy . . . I'm sorry if I hurt your feelings. I'm sorry for what I said. You're great with the horses. And I'm grateful for your help."

Iggy glances at Leo. He snorts, nods at her. She rolls her eyes.

"These sweet horses hate disagreements," she says. "They don't like it when people fight."

"How *do* you know so much about them?"

Iggy grins, just a little. "Secrets, as I said. Everybody's got 'em."

"Ah. Well, like I said, sorry. And Iggy's a great name. Iggy Thump—it sounds brave and bold, like your Papa said."

"Mallie's a good name, too," Iggy says with a grimace. As if it pains her to give a compliment. "That's the name of a moon, you know. Before the Dust came, when winter was finally over, a second moon used to rise in the sky. The Mallie Moon—it was bright and pale pink and people'd dance around in the light when they saw it. Meant winter was over. The blooming season was back. It fits you, I reckon."

This is a bona fide compliment. I'm not sure how to respond exactly. Somehow my hand ended up over my heart while she was talking, like my body reacted to these sweet words of its own accord.

"Oh, please!" Iggy says. "Don't go getting sentimental. You've got a big mission ahead of you."

Three more missions, I think to myself. *Three completed missions, and Denver is safe.*

The mountain of Truth and Flame is a place we've only heard of in stories. It's not visible from the train down the mountain, not even on a clear day. If you travel into the South Woods as far as you can, make it all the way to the cliffs, then you might see a hint of it in the far distance. The mountain is black as char, with flames bursting out the side. Instead of the usual Dust surrounding it, you also have smoke to deal with. It makes for excellent stories, the kind we tell by firelight when winter sets in. We talk about the days before the Dust, when people ventured beyond the mountain we know. Truth and Flame makes for a mighty tale.

But I doubt it's going to be an easy ride.

Also, I have no clue how we're supposed to scrape gold powder from the sides.

We take off from the clearing again and fly south in unison. The flight is long, so we pace our horses. They'll have enough to worry about when we actually get there. We fly for miles. After a while, the peaks around us become unfamiliar-looking, black and forbidding.

"You worried?" Adam yells, flying up beside me.

"A little more than before, maybe," I tell him honestly. "Are you?"

"I'm still rattled from last night," he admits. "I've never seen a monster that close. So much for Mortimer and the Guardians being there to protect us."

I nod and say nothing else. It feels strange holding back something like this. But what would I say? That I possibly saw Mortimer create a *monster*? If I make Mortimer angry, he might let me go. I might lose my place here, even lose the money I've made so far. I can't do it.

"Mallie," Adam calls out. I glance to the side to see the fear on his face as he looks straight ahead, toward the mountain rising dark as a demon miles in front of us.

Truth and Flame.

"Everybody be careful!" Greer calls, flying up on my other side. I see Nico and Connor flying out beside him, focused straight ahead.

I lean forward. "Go, Leo." I say the words against his neck. And say a little prayer that we'll be okay.

In seconds, the world around me is blazing. I can't breathe for the heat of it all.

Smoke billows at my face.

Fire nips my boots, singes the hem of my pants. Leo veers into a hard right, jolting my body, as a plume of fire bursts from the side of the mountain. Sweat beads on my face instantly from the heat. Leo weaves in and out of the smoke, and I squint through my goggles, finally seeing a shimmer.

"I'm ready," I tell Leo, bracing my legs against his sides and unhooking my Keep. Leo flies at an angle up the side of the mountain. I make sure my right arm is through the reins, hooked at the elbow, while I lean down and collect gold powder in my Keep with my left hand. Sweat beads on my forehead and drips down my face. I can hear the deep rumble of the mountain, like it's about to burst all over.

Got it! I pull my Keep away from the mountain, encouraged by the weight of it.

Leo rises into the sky so I can breathe regular air. Even Dusty air feels nice when you're stuck in smoke.

There's still room for more, I think as I look into my Keep.

"Down," I tell Leo. And my brave mount zooms back toward the mountain.

With the bag in hand, I lean low, ready to gather up a pile of gold powder. But Leo swerves suddenly as a flame shoots up out of the mountain so close to my face I wonder if I'm actually burnt.

I remember Iggy's advice about this: Trust Leo completely.

My horse has a knack for knowing when the fire will burst from that mountain. As we make another pass, I see that his instinct is spot-on—swerving, rising, even stomping out flames to keep us safe.

I lean low and collect a final pile of gold powder to top off my Keep. I'm sure there are ashes in this bag, too, but I also know there's gold.

More than enough.

"We did it!" I shout excitedly. "Let's go home, Leo." He swerves and sails skyward.

My hand and Popsnap are covered in soot, and I know that means the rest of me is, too. I smell smoke everywhere: in my hair, in Leo's hair, all around me.

I gulp at the fresh air as Leo bursts out of the smoke cloud surrounding the peaks. Then I check my Keep again. It's full. I wait for the rest of the boys to emerge from the smoke, and my worry sails away, easy as a Starbird in the wind.

Even through the fire, I know I've grabbed enough gold powder to complete today's mission. My whole body feels less tense suddenly. I had a good ride. And maybe because it was so hard, I feel even prouder of myself. I'll have two thousand Feathersworth now. Two more rides and Denver is safe from the mines. My family is safe.

I rest my face on Leo's mane as Adam flies up beside me.

He's covered in soot, too: his hair, his face, even his clothes. We must look like flying shadows. He nods at me, and without even speaking, I know he means two things:

He's safe.

He got enough gold powder, too.

For a few minutes, we soar in circles around each other. We're covered in ashes. We're drifting like shadows. My best friend looks like a warrior, I think, as I watch him sail around me. And I know I must look that way to him, too. It's a fine feeling.

We sigh with relief as we leave Truth and Flame Mountain in our wake.

Leo and I land in the clearing behind Greer, just before Adam. Before Leo is even fully on the ground, I'm swinging off his back to check for injuries.

"You were so brave," I tell him, kissing his sooty muzzle.

I ruffle Leo's mane, shaking the smoke loose from the green stripe that matches mine. He touches his muzzle to my forehead.

"Lionhearted Leo," I whisper. "That's what you are."

And his deep brown eyes are on my eyes. It's like he hugs me with his eyes sometimes. Leo can't speak, of course, but I still feel like he communicates with me. Like there's an unspoken understanding between us. Sometimes just looking into his eyes makes me feel brave, too. *You are the lionhearted one*, his heart seems to be saying to mine. *You are brave.*

"I'm brave when you're with me." I grin.

Iggy scuttles up beside us, muttering to herself, scanning Leo for burns I might have missed. Of course, she couldn't care less if I'm hurt. But she's endlessly concerned for "her" horses. This is becoming very endearing to me.

She sighs and pats his side. "All's good with sweet Leo, it seems. I'll take him to the stable for dinner and a bath." Iggy doesn't actually have stables set up in the West Woods. But there is a grove of Telling Trees she calls her stables. There's a little creek and plenty of shade, and she insists the horses are left alone when they go there. All animals need rest, she says. "I'll take Jeff, too, Adam."

The horses follow Iggy happily, ready for some alone time with her. But I know Leo will find me later.

"I'm too riled up to go straight home," Adam says, as if he's reading my mind. "There's something I want to show you. Meet me back here after they weigh our powder, okay?"

"Don't look up yet!" Adam insists as he guides me down a new path in the West Woods. I don't have to see to know we're deep in the forest: The ground is brambly, the wind is whispering in the trees, the night birds are already tweeting faintly.

"We have to get home soon," I remind him, as if he doesn't know. The Feathersworth are jingling in my bag and I can't wait to give them to Mama. I can't wait to show them what I've done.

"We have plenty of time," he assures me. "This is worth it."

The path narrows, and I lean in closer to him. I know I'm brave. I've proved it to everybody—and to myself— more than once now. But this unknown place still scares me. If flying has taught me anything, it's that it's possible to be brave and afraid at the same time. One always leads to another.

"Okay," Adam says, leading me into a circular grove in the middle of tall, thin trees. "Don't look up! Just sit down slowly."

I do and then follow his lead and lie back on the soft grass beside him.

"Look at that," he whispers.

I don't understand why he's whispering—we're all alone out here. But when I see what he's looking at, everything makes sense. This is a reverent moment. As magic as anything I've ever seen.

The bare branches of Telling Trees stretch over us. And dangling from those branches like leaves—I see shiny Starpatches.

I gasp. At first, I say nothing. I watch the veins of color and light flicker across those patches. Watch them flutter, go nearly invisible, then bright again.

A strange impulse rises up in me: to cry, to celebrate, to be still. All of that at once. All I feel is wonder. I'm not seeing a rogue Starpatch floating through the open window. I'm seeing a bunch of them—enough to make a whole blanket, maybe. My fingertips are itching to touch them. To feel them. To make them into something.

"How did you find these?" I whisper.

"It sounds crazy, but I felt like . . . I heard them. Like there was this buzz of energy coming from over here, and there they were."

"Do you think they're new?" I ask. "Are the stars finding a way back in? Is the light coming back?"

This would be a better answer to our worries than gold powder. We would have a better way to make a living. The sadness in our eyes would vanish with starlight on our shoulders. The mines would be boarded up and closed; we wouldn't even need them anymore.

"I hope so," Adam says. "That'd be like a miracle, wouldn't it? If the light found a way in?"

"It would," I say, watching them flicker and shine.

Night is close, so Adam lights the lanterns we carried with us. We set them to flicker on the soft grass. I watch the light shimmer across the Starpatches and remember the place where I met Leo. It was a meadow like this. And it felt as magical as this moment does, lying on our backs staring up through the branches at the Dusty skies.

Tell him, my heart says. Tell him about the Dustsnake Mortimer made. Some animals—and humans—are worth trusting with your whole heart, always. As I turn my face to speak, I see him drawing with his finger in the dirt.

Familiar memories of Adam drift through my mind: him scribbling on scrap pieces of paper or in notebooks, drawing in the dust on the sides of buildings. When we were kids, he always had pictures in his mind. He couldn't wait to get them out.

"So, you still draw?" I ask.

"In my dreams, mostly. Sometimes on breaks Down Below I paint on the walls with water and coal dust. I'm out of practice, though."

I roll back my sleeve and offer my arm. "Here. Paint my universal orange Popsnap. Something that will help me remember I'm a fierce flier."

He mixes Dust and water and goes to work making vines, flowers, Honeysuckle swooping, Leo flying, a small flower.

"What's the flower for?"

"Gentle things are fierce, too," he reminds me. And I wonder if he's heard my mama say that, or if he just believes it.

His brush gently dances over the Popsnap as he draws a star, dripping, a line leading down to an inky heart.

"I know there's something you want to tell me," he says finally.

"How do you know?"

"You're never ever quiet unless you have something big on your mind."

I glance around the clearing to make sure we weren't followed. I keep my voice as low and breathe: "I don't think that monster the other night was real. I saw Mortimer make that thing, that snake, to scare Honor's friends. It was . . . a Dustpuppet, kind of. I don't know how else to describe it."

"Mortimer *made* it?"

"Yes," I whisper. "Just spun it right up out of the dirt. That's what it looked like, at least."

There's a prickling sensation against my neck, like I'm being watched. I glance over my shoulder, but see nothing.

"So, wait." Adam's inky eyes connect with mine. "You saw him do it . . . and you didn't say anything?"

"I wasn't really sure what I saw," I explain quickly.

And then Adam's eyes go wide with a warning. He's looking over my shoulder, into the woods behind me.

"What a marvelous discovery, children."

We leap off the ground at the sound of Mortimer's voice. I've been caught. I know it. I just spilled Mortimer's secret. Fear surges through me.

Did he hear what we just said? He doesn't appear to have. He looks delighted by the sight of the Starpatches in the trees.

"Adam found them," I tell him. "Do you think the Starpatches are slipping through the Dust somehow? Do you think they've found a way?"

Mortimer's smile tightens ever so slightly. "I wish that were true, Mallie. But the Dust snuffed out the stars. It's a lovely thought, though. The two of you should head back to Coal Top before the night sets in. Wouldn't want you to feel unsafe on the path."

Adam isn't saying anything in response to Mortimer. He's just glaring at him, in a way that's far too obvious. I tug Adam's shirt. "Come on. Let's walk home."

Adam nods, and we walk away together, very aware of the fact that Mortimer is watching us go.

When we're deep enough in the woods, Adam grabs my wrist.

"Stop," he whispers. And he nods his head toward the way we've come. "I want to see what he does with them."

We're nearly silent as we walk back, lurking behind trees, fading into the shadows easily. By the time we're back at the Telling Trees, the Guardians are there with him. One of them is carrying a small torch. Mortimer isn't smiling at the Starpatches anymore.

"None of the kids have been singing, have they?" Mortimer says to the Guardian holding the flame, so softly that I barely hear.

"No, sir," the man confirms. "We won't allow it."

Mortimer responds by nodding toward the trees.

He walks away, and Adam and I watch in disbelief as Mortimer's men take their swords and stab the patches, pulling them down from the trees. One by one, they feed the Starpatches to the Guardian's flame. The light flickers, then curls as it burns, black and singed, falling as ashes to the ground.

Taken

Adam and I trudge toward home together.

"Why would he do that?" I ask in a shaky voice. I'm surprised by the heavy sadness in my stomach. Maybe anger is what I should be feeling right now. "Why would he burn the Starpatches?"

"Why would he create a monster?" Adam shakes his head. "People told me I shouldn't trust Mortimer. I know

I can't trust the Guardians, but I guess I thought he was different."

I tell Adam about Mama's similar warning. We talk as we walk, and soon enough Connor and Nico join us. We tell them everything we've seen in the past few days. We're so fired up talking that I don't see Greer running toward us. He always beats all of us home. He's small but he's fast. Today, he's doubled back to meet us.

"Go home, Mallie," he says. The wild gleam in his eyes sends a bolt of fear through my body. "Granny Mab told me to find you. Hurry home. Now."

I'm running already, faintly aware of Adam calling out my name. I know I've never moved faster than this, never longed more for my own set of wings to fly to the people I love. I round the path expecting to see the cottage ahead.

But I'm slammed nearly to a stop by a cloud of Dust.

Bursts of breath erupt from my lungs as I fight through the haze. Where did this come from? I pull my scarf up over my nose so I don't breathe it in—the Dust makes me angry, makes me lose focus. I have to stay focused now.

My heart sinks when I see the front door wide open.

The sound of my parents' soft sobbing feels as loud as thunder in the Lightning Range.

The furniture is all overturned. A window is broken. The Dust is hazy, purple-looking, yellow at the edges— thick enough to push away. Mama and Papa are slumped onto the floor, holding each other. Honeysuckle's perched on Papa's shoulder, her head bowed. She isn't singing. She has nothing to sing for today.

Mama reaches her hand to me, and I take it, thinking she wants me to pull her up. But she doesn't move.

"Where'd they take him? And why'd they come early?" I ask. "I'll get him right now. Tell me!"

But Mama shakes her head.

Pulls me down onto the floor.

Papa's hand is on my arm, too. And they're both looking at me with vacant, hopeless eyes. I'm breathing in so much Dust; it's all around me. It's disarming today. It burns my nose and my lungs with every breath. I can feel my shoulders slumping.

It's as if the floors of my house are quicksand, pulling me in. And I'm not even fighting to get up.

Denver is gone.

His absence is a weight on my chest that I can't lift off. It's crushing me.

"It's too late, Mallie," Mama says. "They came for him."

"Mallie?" Adam's voice at the door.

I don't even know how long I've been sitting here. Minutes? Hours?

His arms are underneath me. "There's so much Dust in here. We've got to get out."

"I feel like I can't move," I tell him.

Somehow he's pulling me to my feet. He loops my arm around his shoulders; we're like the men we saw on the platform. "I'll move with you," he says. His voice feels far away. "I'm here with you. One step at a time."

His friends rush into the room around us—Connor, Nico, and Greer. Greer holds Honeysuckle close to his chest, softly petting her tiny head as he hurries her out of the house. Nico and Connor help my parents. Step by step.

"Don't breathe this in," Adam warns them.

"This is worse than the Dust in the mines," I hear Nico say.

We burst into fresh air and slump down in the dewy grass.

"Deep breaths," Adam tells me. His voice is a low rumble. "I've heard the Guardians do this sometimes, when they search. Add extra Dust to the house. It's worse than a Dustblob in the trees. Breathe in too much and it makes you feel . . ."

Nothing. I feel like nothing, and there's really no way to describe how nothing feels.

The longer we're outside, the stronger I feel. And as the minutes pass, I see life coming back into my parents' eyes. Life, and—with that—sorrow.

Because Dust or no Dust, my brother is gone. There's no worse sadness than that.

The Dust has barely cleared from the house when we hear the familiar sound of Granny Mab's cart.

I run for her, but I don't have to say anything. By the look in her eyes, I can see that she knows.

"I saw him at the platform," Granny Mab tells me, quietly, so my parents can't hear.

"They didn't even wait a week! They lied." My left hand curls into a fist. Hope and fury surge through me, twist around inside me. "Is he hurt?"

She shakes her head. "He stood there with some other little ones. He was holding an old stuffed bear and a book. He had a baby Dustflight on his shoulder."

She clutches my shoulders with her long, bony fingers and looks right into my eyes. "His little chest was puffed in pride, Mallie. He wasn't about to cry."

Tears sting my eyes. "Because he thinks I'll fix everything."

"He's right," Granny Mab says, eyebrow raised. "I know which mine he's in—"

"Tell me!" I beg. "I can go get him! Tonight! Leo will take me and—"

"Shhh," Mab cautions. "He was sorted at the platform and sent to the mine up here, the mountain mine. The same one your father worked at. But hear me out now, Mallie. If you try to rescue him tonight . . . try to take him out of the mines, you'll be an outlaw."

"They'll never catch me," I tell her. "Leo will take us far away from here."

"What about your parents? Adam's parents? I know you see the answer, Mallie. You're a bright girl. Finish your last few missions. Pay off the debt. He'll be home straightaway."

"I can't fly if I know he's Down Below. I won't."

"You can," Granny Mab assures me. "And I brought something to help you." She motions for me to walk around to the other side of her cart.

A lonesome wind pushes the trees back and forth around me. The smell of rain is in the air: rain, and smoke, and Dust. My eyes still burn from my time in the cottage. I still feel weak when I walk.

Mab tosses a few scary-looking dolls off the cart, rummaging for whatever she has for me. "Ah! Here we go. One package for Miss Mallie."

I shake my head. "I don't want it. I don't want anything right now."

"Mab," Mama says, standing in front of us. I didn't even hear her approaching. "If you're trying to sell us something after this, you can leave and not come back."

I raise my eyebrows. Mama is definitely not being gentle right now.

"You think I'm that low?" Granny Mab asks. "That false-hearted? No. This is a gift."

Mama nods and wraps her arms around her chest. Her eyes are red from tears.

Granny Mab nods to me. "This is from one of her admirers. People are telling stories about her all over the mountain, you know. Mallie over the Moon. She's their hero."

"She's too brave for her own good," Mama says. It's the closest she's come to saying she's proud of me. It settles on my heart the same way.

"I remember another girl that same way." Granny Mab raises an eyebrow matter-of-factly.

I glance quickly at my mother. What's that supposed to mean?

Mama says nothing. I realize now that Mama's silence is full of stories, full of words unspoken.

Granny Mab holds the box out for me. It's wrapped in brown paper, tied with a white twine bow.

I hold the package steady with my right arm and work the knot loose with my left hand. When I flip the lid, something inside sparkles. The dull shine is so sudden, so unexpected, that I squint as I reach into the box. The object is cold, and metal, and almost feels like fingers. I dig deeper to see.

"Is this a Popsnap?" I ask. It looks nothing like any I've ever seen before. It's silver—metallic and shiny. Every joint of every finger bends. And looks as if it's the perfect size for me, made to connect comfortably to my arm. Even without trying it on, I can tell it's going to fit better.

"Where'd you get this?" I ask.

Granny Mab grins. "I know the timing is bad, but it's been on order for a while. As I said, it comes from someone who is proud of you. There's a card in there."

For Mallie over the Moon,
my champion. My star.

"*Someone* must have special-ordered it for you from a craftsman in the valley," Granny Mab says. "I don't know who. I'm just the delivery girl."

But I know who sent it as soon as I study the note. The

handwriting is a giveaway, the way the letters slant and loop so gently.

"Mama?" I ask, looking at her face for assurance. "You gave me this?"

Her face is still shiny with tears. Eyes still red from all the Dust. "I thought it was time for a better one," she says. "Show her how it works, Mab."

"Oh!" I say as Granny Mab quickly maneuvers one finger into a small beam of light. It doesn't just grab, bend, and hold like a hand. Every finger has a tool inside it.

"All you do," Granny Mab tells me, "is reach over, flip, and there you have it."

I pull off my orange Popsnap and hand it to Mama. The metallic one seems to mold to me. I flick at the fingers and find a knife, a tiny pair of pliers, and a measuring stick. The silver thumb is hollow.

"For money," Granny Mab qualifies. "Or love notes."

She wiggles her eyebrows, and it's so cheesy, I laugh a little—for the first time since I got home.

"It's made of lava rock from Mirror Mountain," Granny Mab says. "That's why it's so shiny. I've sold the rocks themselves in my carts before. They're strong, but they can still be moved and molded. It'll come in especially handy for your missions."

Or for pulling my brother out of some terrible mine, I think.

In my heart, I know that Granny Mab is probably right. The missions are all I can do for now. I just need two more, and then I'll free my brother from the mine. And then I'll keep riding, keep flying, until we have no more worries at all. Until I have enough to make a better story for all of us.

I flick the fingers of my new Popsnap—my UtilitySnap—back into place. It's weird but wonderful, too, this silver hand. *My* silver hand.

Denver will love this.

A low-flying wave of Dust sails past me, unexpectedly. I breathe it in, and close my eyes. Denver. I shape the fingers of the UtilitySnap into a fist.

"Mallie," Granny Mab says, a warning in her voice. "Remember what we talked about."

"I won't forget," I promise her. But even as the Dust passes away, the sorrow in my soul gives way to anger. I won't forget what they've done.

19

Secrets and Smoke

There is no Dust.

There is dull yellow light—cold but bright enough burn away every Dustblob in the trees. Standing here in the woods, I hear those patches sizzling all around me. Ashes fall like snow.

"Mallie!"

Denver is up ahead in the woods, waving me toward him. He's okay. Nothing happened! The scene at the house was only a nightmare, and he's okay. I run after him, calling out his name.

The ashes fall thicker around me. The light begins to dim in the sky. "Wait," I call out to my brother. Again, louder: "Wait for me!"

But he's fast, and my legs are moving as if they're stuck in bog water, mud thick all around me. A *whoosh* and something flies over me—crows, I think. I hear them caw. See their black feathers. But as soon as they land, those feathers bloom into capes, and there are no birds. Only Guardians. One of them holds my brother by the arm. Tears streak down Denver's dusty face.

And I can't speak now.

My voice is gone, like Papa's.

A scream wild inside me—an eruption of sound— boils in my heart, but all that comes out is a silent roar as they drag him away. And then I'm tossed over an edge I didn't see, still unable to scream, clawing the air for something—anything—to hold.

"NO!" I gasp, and sit up in my bed. Darkness mostly fills my room, but Mama left a lantern flickering on my dresser. I know the window is open because I feel the cool wind, and because my throat is scratchy from breathing in the Dust. I stand and push my sweaty hair away from my face, holding the lantern up to Denver's bed.

Maybe it was all a bad dream—every second of it.

But there's no little boy in the bunk above me. Only a sad yellow bird, nestled on his pillow asleep.

I hear a soft animal's snort from the window and look up to see Leo's face shining in the light.

Running to him, I lift my arms around his strong, muscular neck, I bury my face in his mane.

As I pull back, Leo touches his muzzle to my tears. The sadness doesn't leave me, but I feel stronger as I hold him. I've always heard people say they own animals. This is *my* Dustflight, *my* dog, *my* pet hedgehog. But this isn't true of my horse: We belong to *each other*.

Riding tomorrow, that's the only way I can save my brother. But if I could just see him, and know that he's okay . . .

"Do you know where the mountain mines are?" I ask Leo in a soft whisper. The horse lifts his head once, as if he's saying yes. Or maybe, *Come with me.*

I climb out the window and onto his back. Leo's demeanor is gentle tonight as we trot into the woods. His wings press extra tight against me, like he's hugging me close.

"Take me to him?" I ask. "Maybe I can even bring him home tonight. Hide him until I have all the money turned in. Then it won't matter, right?"

There's a hesitation in my horse; I can feel it. But he breaks into a run, then leaps, then soars up through the trees and into the night. We fly together high above the woods, where no monsters can reach us. Where no Guardians can take away the people we love. Here between the Dust and the ground, life never seems as scary.

But the Dust is wild tonight.

I cough as Leo zooms through the middle of a low-flying cloud of the stuff.

And again, rage consumes me. I want to hurt those Guardians for taking my brother.

I will hurt them.

Claw their eyes out and scream in their faces.

I'll roar louder than any monster they'll ever encounter.

I want to scream at Mortimer Good. I'm one of his best riders. He oversees the mines . . . and *he* still let the Guardians come for Denver? I wonder what he would feel like in the Down Below when rocks start falling, when the birds cry out warnings of an explosion.

And then . . . almost as soon as the rage fogs over my mind, Leo pivots, flying out of the Dustcloud. The anger doesn't dissolve completely, but I don't feel over-whelmed by it.

The Dust, I realize now, makes me horrible.

The Dust is a villain I don't know how to fight.

The Coal Top mine is a short flight from my house. It's looked the same since I was a girl, since I went to take Papa his lunch or watch for him to come home in the afternoons. The mines have always been there, but they haven't always been evil. For as long as the mountain has been here, we've loved to explore it, care for the rare stones inside it, study the strange creatures who live and thrive down in the darkness. There are lizards in the mines that change color with the seasons. There are caverns with lakes. Papa took me to one of those once, a lake under a ceiling of bats that sleep all across the top of the cavern. Their wings glow in the darkness, giving light to the water. "Just because a creature loves the night doesn't mean it's bad," Papa told me.

I cling to this memory. Because the mines are different now. The darkness is so thick down there that it disorients people, especially at first. And the smells are foul. The smell of the Dust is bad enough. But there's a rotten, eggy smell that belches up out of the mines the deeper down you go. And somewhere down there, in all that dark and stink, my brother is alone. He's clinging to an old teddy bear and a scared little bird, waiting for me.

"I'm coming, Denver," I whisper.

Two Guardians wait at the mine entrance, holding lanterns. So Leo and I fly high above the tree line to avoid detection. He sails above the mine, landing in a patch of grass underneath the trees. I swing off Leo's back to get a better look at my surroundings. The mine is below me somewhere. I just need a way inside.

"There's got to be another door," I say to Leo. He doesn't react at all. Because he's not paying attention to me.

Leo's head is dipped low, his nostrils are flared. He's looking deep into the woods.

I round in front of my horse to protect him. With a hard nudge of his nose, Leo pushes me out of the way and gets in front of me.

"Mallie?"

I feel an invisible weight lift from my shoulders. Relief shoots through my veins so fast, I nearly collapse to the ground. It's just Adam. Adam and his horse, Jeff. Adam leads Jeff out of the woods and keeps his eye on me. Leo trots over to Jeff, and they gently bump foreheads.

"What are you doing here?" I whisper-yell.

"I could ask you the same thing! I flew over to check on you, and you were gone. I had a feeling this is where you'd be. You can't bust him out, Mallie! You'll be thrown out of the missions for good. Why are you being so stubborn?"

"He needs me," I say. "I know it. I can't leave him here. If I take him home tonight and complete the mission tomorrow, it will all be all right. They'll just think he ran away."

"They don't like runaways," Adam warns me. "And there's no way inside. There's one entrance to the mountain mine."

I shake my head. "I don't believe that. The Guardians would give themselves more than one way out, wouldn't they? Surely you've seen them leave through more than just the front door."

Adam frowns. "I don't pay much attention, really. I just try to do what they tell me, just finish for the day."

I do the same thing, I realize. And it occurs to me now that we all do this—everybody on the mountain. We don't question anything. We must live the stories we're given. That's what we're told, so that's what we do. When did we stop questioning things?

A cool wind trills across the ground, and I shiver. "What do you think Denver's doing now?"

Adam hesitates. "There's a big cave where new recruits sleep, deep in the center of the mine. Little nooks are carved into the walls, just big enough for a blanket and pillow. They're all together in there. It's not as bad as it seems."

I don't realize I've started crying again until I feel a tear drip off my chin. Also, I laugh, but not because I think any of this is funny. " 'Recruit.' As if anybody would choose this. There's got to be another way in!"

Adam holds up his hand. "Keep your voice down. This place is swarming with Guardians."

Ignoring Adam, I turn to the horses. "Jeff. Leo. Fly over and see if you can find us another way inside. Go."

The horses hesitate, but they listen. They swoop up and over us, wings steady. I know how loud a Starbird can be, but I'm almost more amazed by how quietly they can move.

"That was a bad idea," Adam says, his voice a frantic whisper. "We're above the mines, there are Guardians everywhere, and our horses are gone."

"They're finding a way in," I tell him. "I just want to see Denver. To see he's okay . . ."

"He's fine!" Adam says. "Don't underestimate how strong your brother is. You owe him that. He never underestimates you."

Adam is right. I can't stop worrying about Denver completely. I guess I never will. But a cool breeze floats between us and lifts some of my worry away with it. My plan isn't working out exactly the way I want, but that doesn't mean it's not working. I'm only two missions away from saving him. And yes, I know he is afraid down there. But I also know he's brave. He's a Ramble, my Ramble.

"You're right," I say, pushing a frazzle of hair out of my face. "I shouldn't have come here. This was stupid. In a few more days, he'll be home. I'll whistle for the horses and we can go."

Adam grabs my arm a little too tight. This close to him, I see fear shine in his eyes.

So low that I can barely hear the words, he mouths: "Be very quiet. Don't move."

Barely louder than my breath, than my heartbeat, I hear the sounds: twigs breaking beneath slow, solid footsteps. A swish across the forest floor.

A low and happy hiss from behind me.

Adam is staring over my shoulder. "I see its eyes," he whispers. "Yellow eyes. I see its . . . teeth."

"Maybe it's only Dust." My reply is soft, quiet as the breeze blowing around us. Chillbumps rise along my arms.

Adam shakes his head, barely. "It doesn't look like Dust."

"Does it see us?"

Adam waits for one breath. Then another. His eyes stay focused on the same spot over my shoulder. With a shaky breath he answers, "Yes."

I turn slowly, so that I'm in front of Adam.

There is a cloud of Dust not fifteen feet away from me. And in that haze, I see the same bright yellow eyes Adam sees. The same eyes I saw in the West Woods the night I met Leo. They're the same color as the eyes of Mortimer's Dustpuppet, only bigger.

I can't make out the shape of the monster, but I see its tail through the cover of dust—swishing back and forth against the ground. Just like a dog, when that dog is about to get a delicious treat.

I feel pinned to the place I'm standing. Sweat beads across my forehead, above my lip. I feel Adam spin, so we're back-to-back. "There are more," he says, his words coming out on a choppy burst of breath.

A hiss from the mist nearby in the woods.

A hiss from the Dust rising up to my left.

Adam's hand grabs for mine, and I wonder if my hand is as cold as his. "There are three of them, Mallie—"

"Don't call for the horses," I whisper. "The Guardians will come for us. I don't want them to hear us scream."

It's a terrible decision to make: Would we rather be caught by Guardians and lose the chance to ride? Or eaten by monsters?

"I have to call for them," Adam says. I feel him trembling against me. Or maybe I'm the one trembling.

"Don't scream," I beg. "We'll be kicked out of the missions."

"I wish you'd thought of that before you came *here*," Adam says.

"You didn't have to follow me!"

We're surrounded by Dust and monster eyes. I hear their claws scrape the ground, their tails sliding.

I want to crumble as those eyes bore into me. They're a hypnotic yellow, a dull fire. The color of my nightmares.

Suddenly, the woods are full of footsteps—the loud steps grown men make. Lanterns beam in the darkness. "Someone's out there." The voice of a Guardian. "The beasts have something!"

"Hold steady," I tell Adam. "The horses will save us."

A wild rush of wind stirs the ground all around me, blowing up a storm of Dust. Leo and Jeff land in the center, and we jump on their backs. One of the monsters leaps through the fog and I see its wolfish face—snapping—snarling at us.

Guardians storm out of the woods, swords drawn, but we're too far now to be seen.

Once we're a safe distance away, Adam yells, "Let's never sneak into the mine again. Or at least let's not get caught next time."

I laugh, a little. But my body is still tense. As my heart steadies, my mind works out a different kind of thought: The Guardians . . . they aren't afraid of these monsters. They came right at them. They control the monsters. The monsters control us.

Iggy was right. Everyone has secrets.

Especially Mortimer Good.

20

The Tale of Iggy Thump

Our next day's mission will take place at the Lightning Range. It's a place of endless storms, Papa told me once. No peace in sight. This is fitting for me. *Endless storms* is exactly how I would describe my mood.

"You've got to calm down," Adam tells me as we saddle our horses.

"I can't. I didn't sleep at all after I got home. I won't

sleep until Denver is out of the mine. I should have rescued him last night."

"Two more missions, and you're good! Stay the course, Mallie," Adam says. "Focus on the missions ahead."

Just the missions. Nothing else. I know he's right. But here's the thing: Worrying about Denver wasn't all that kept me awake last night. I thought about the monsters and the Guardians and how they weren't afraid of them. That unsettled me as much as the monsters themselves. I thought about Mortimer Good, how he spun one up out of the Dust. And I thought about how it was time for someone—maybe me—to start asking questions. I want to know how Mortimer's strange web connects together. And I think I know someone who can help me . . . if she will.

Out of the corner of my eye, I see a tiny mushroom girl feeding carrots to a blue-maned horse called Fiyero.

"Stay," I say to Leo, petting his muzzle. I walk casually over where Iggy is talking—baby-talking, actually—to Fiyero. She might act tough on the outside, but she's got a soft and tender heart.

"Iggy." I come to a stop behind her. She stops talking to the horse, but she doesn't turn toward me. "I don't mean to interrupt, but I need to ask you a question."

Iggy still doesn't turn as she holds out another

bright orange carrot for the horse. "I'm having an important conversation with Fiyero, Mallie-girl. Can it wait for a bit?"

"No," I say quietly, so only she can hear. "I don't think it can. Do you remember when you told me that I didn't know what it was like to miss someone? I do now. The Guardians took my brother last night."

Iggy goes still. Her stance softens as she turns toward me. "I'm sorry for that." She looks at the ground and shakes her head. "I am sorry. From the truest place in my heart, I'm sorry. Wish I could help."

"You can, I think." I kneel down, reaching for a carrot to feed the horse. I don't want the Guardians thinking we're talking about anything important.

"You told me once that everybody has secrets. I need to know yours. Especially if you know secrets about Mortimer Good."

"Shhh," Iggy cautions. "Don't say his name so loud. Even if I do know things"—she glances around and adds, almost silently—"which I do, I can't tell 'em to you. I've got someone to protect, too, see. I'm sorry about your brother, though."

I lean closer and whisper, "I know Mortimer is doing something bad. Talk to me for the sake of the animals. I know you love the horses. Let's start there. I want to

223

know how he brought them back. And why he brought them back."

Fury sparks in her eyes. "He didn't bring 'em back. I did."

Iggy glances down at her wrinkly boots as soon as she realizes what she's said. She knows she's let too much information slip.

"Please," I beg. "I'll never tell anyone that you've told me. But I might have to do something dangerous really soon. I need your help."

She's chewing on her lip. Pondering her options.

"Iggy?"

She presses her tiny fist to her forehead and sighs. "Meet me at the stables in a bit. Quick like. Before I change my mind and before the mission starts."

Iggy's "stables" are even prettier than she described them. Tall Telling Trees form a protective hedge around a tiny clearing, rolling down toward a creek sprinkled with lily pads.

"The horses like to take baths in that creek," she says, walking me to a spot far enough to prevent any nosy Guardian from hearing our conversation. "Sometimes at night, I sit on this stump right here and they gather around for me to read them stories. Animals love a good book, you know."

"I know Dustflights do," I say, thinking about all the times I've seen Honeysuckle reading over Papa's and Denver's shoulders. The memory is a sharp pain in my heart. "So what I need to know is—"

"I'll tell you what you need to know," she says with a huff. "Head for that Willow Tree over there. Willow Trees are the best for serious conversations. They'll hold a person's secrets. Toss 'em around in the branches until they sound like a pretty rattle. You can always trust horses and trees."

"How did you bring the horses back?" I ask when we're safe beneath the shade of the Willow.

"I'll make it as quick as I can, Mallie-girl: My papa and I, we lived here in the West Woods, see. We were hiding from the Guardians. Papa worked in the mines for a bit, but they said he messed up some equipment."

"Mine, too!" I say with a gasp. "They accused my father of the same thing. I know they're lying."

Iggy nods. "That's why Papa and I hid in the West Woods."

I stare at her in disbelief. "Weren't you afraid of the monsters?"

Iggy snorts like I've told a joke. "Strange things, those monsters. When I first came here, I hid from them. I used to tremble when I heard them stomping around at night. In the day, too, sometimes. Then I came face-to-face with one. They're terrible creatures. The one I saw had a body like a wolf. Face like a snake. Like somebody took a nightmare right out of my brain and dropped it on the path in front of me. I was stuck. I knew I couldn't run from it; my legs are too short, see? So, I stood my ground. And screamed in its face."

"You *yelled* at it?"

Iggy shrugs. "It's all I could think to do! And here's the truth; it left me alone. I wasn't so afraid of them after that. They look terrifying, those monsters. But . . ."

Iggy's voice trails off. I finish for her: "They're not real. None of them?"

Iggy shakes her head slowly: nope. "The Guardians all know how to make them. I don't know why they do it." My breath hitches. Even though I suspected this, *saw* this, the reality of it makes me feel shaky.

A thought I've been tossing around for days finally makes its way to the surface: "Because if you can make someone afraid, they listen to you. They obey you."

A loud shout comes from the clearing. The Guardians are gathering everyone up for the mission.

"Quickly," I say. "Tell me how you brought the Starbirds back. How you met Mortimer."

"I love my papa more than anybody in the world; he's my dearest friend. The finest dad. But I got a little lonely out here without anyone else. Nobody to play with, see. So one day I was crying all by my lonesome, underneath a Telling Tree. And that's when a Starbird found me."

Iggy's eyes glisten at the memory. "I used to ride him—Fred, I called him—through the woods. Papa told me not to go too far. We don't want to get caught, he said. But I couldn't help it . . . every day we rode a little farther. A little farther. One day I was caught by the Guardians."

I imagine the Guardians' eyes when they saw a Starbird for the first time in years. The thought of them being afraid gives me a little burst of delight.

"They took my horse away," Iggy continues. "Put me in a room alone, and I didn't know what they'd do with me. Or how my papa must be worrying. Finally, in walks Mortimer Good with steaming-hot food and fresh cocoa and says he's there to help me. 'Lead me to the Starbirds,' he says. 'I just want to see them. Lead me to the Starbirds and I'll give your horse back. I'll take you back to your papa.' So, I show him the Starbirds, and then he says to train them, to keep them in the West Woods. 'Work for me,' he says, 'and you won't be punished for hiding out here in the woods without permission. And once you've done good enough work, you can go home to your papa.'

Now . . . I'm stuck, see? I won't see Papa again until Mortimer Good says I've done good work. Then he'll return me to my family."

"He has your papa and your horse?" I ask, my body tensing like I'm ready to pounce. It's a good thing Mortimer Good's not standing here in front of me right now. I am not in a gentle mood.

"That's right." Iggy nods. "But I've got secrets, too. He could take all these horses away from me if he wanted, but I'll always be connected to them."

Iggy pulls off her mushroom hat and thick cascades of braided black hair come tumbling down. Each braid has a different color twisted up inside it, but the thickest color, the most prominent, is a vibrant shade of pink. "And they're all connected to me," she says. "They take care of me, even now."

Standing under the Willow, rainbow hair falling down around her shoulders, Iggy Thump looks like she's fallen out of a storybook. She looks like a little mountain queen. Full of good secrets.

Iggy smiles sadly. "The horses won't leave this mountain as long as children need them. They never left the mountain. But we did—we went into the mines and into the valleys. And they waited, here, in the woods, where people used to come and ride them. Mortimer doesn't have to worry about these horses going anywhere. He never did."

A silver tear slides down Iggy's face. "Mortimer found a way to make it all work for him, though. He always does. The rich get richer. The poor get poorer. And he keeps dangling hope down in front of us like some crunchy golden carrot. We keep putting our trust in him because he's a smooth talker. But he's not to be trusted. We must live the stories we're given," Iggy says, rolling her eyes. "That's what the Guardians tell us. They say the Dust is poison if we sing, and we believe it. They say the Dust snuffed out the stars, and we believe it."

"We don't question it," I add, my voice rising like a Starbird into the sky.

"Right! Everybody just carries on, believing everything they're told. And it's 'cause we're all desperate to protect people—and animals—that we love. That's true for me. Describes you, too, I think."

I nod. It is true of me. "I'm going to help you get your horse back, Iggy."

Iggy shakes her head. "If you try, he'll hurt my sweet horse. He'll hurt Fred. I told you the truths I know, but that's all I can do, Mallie-girl. I'm brave, but in a different way than you."

Maybe in a better way, I think. Suddenly, it's not so hard for me to picture this small girl screaming in the face of a monster. Maybe I need to start doing that, too.

Sometimes it's better to sing instead of scream.

But maybe sometimes it's okay to roar.

Iggy shoos me back out of her stables toward the clearing. When I look back, I see her sitting in the grass beside the creek, braiding a crown of daisies to add to her rainbow hair. The horses kneel down around her, surrounding her. Iggy the brave. Iggy their queen.

Mortimer strides into the middle of the clearing. He isn't dressed in a velvet blazer today; he's wearing a slick black jacket made for rain. Silver buttons gleaming. Riding boots shining. His clothes don't impress me anymore. The sight of his face makes me clench my fist.

I'm surprised when he turns toward us. There's a storm brewing in his eyes. Something has him rattled today.

"Today's mission is in the Lightning Range," Mortimer says, scraping his fingers through his hair. "You'll battle the elements, certainly. But I hope you'll refrain from battling one another. I've heard things get nasty when you're out on missions. Don't let anger get the best of you, my riders." He glances between Honor and me. "Today's mission will be just a little bit different. I'll let Iggy give you specifics. Then I'll tell you about today's . . . twist."

Iggy marches in front of him, hands on hips, looking around. Her hat is back in place, hiding all the rainbow strands. "Well, like the boss just said, you'll be working the Lightning Range today. This is the most dangerous range you've tread so far. There's only one way to handle it—you trust your horse. Horses have instincts, see. They'll know how to dodge those fire bolts. They understand the sky. They're built to crack the wind with their wings."

Mortimer nods but says nothing, like he's trying to pick exactly the right words to say next. The confident shine in his eyes is replaced by another look, a hungry look. Like the gleam in the eyes of the monsters. "The Lightning Range is vital in other ways, children. You'll be given an extra Keep today. And I want you to use it to look for something besides gold powder."

I glance at Adam and he shrugs his shoulders. Even Iggy looks confused.

Mortimer waves a Guardian to his side. The man is holding a small brown bag. Similar to the bags they use to give us our Feathersworth. He opens the sack and walks around for us to see.

My eyebrows scrunch closer at the sight of what's inside.

It's the dull yellow powder, the kind I saw back at the Tumbrels. The kind I see on my boots sometimes. A dull yellow like the dust of our earth, like the morning sky, like my nightmares, even.

"This is Timor powder," Mortimer says gravely. "We use this mineral in our medicine. As you know, the mines get more dangerous the deeper we get. And we're running low on resources to keep our miners safe. Gold powder isn't all we're after."

Strange, I think. Gold powder is all he's cared about until now.

"So we're all depending on you to bring back Timor. It's especially prevalent where storms are brewing, where lightning strikes and scorches the ground." Something about the way he says this sends a shiver down my spine. "The rider who brings back the most Timor powder today will earn an extra five hundred Feathersworth. This could change everything for some of you."

Mortimer Good stares directly at me. "One decision can change everything."

A shiver rakes across my ribs. He's warning me, I realize. Does he know what I've seen? Is he daring me not to tell?

What if I do tell everyone? What if expose his lies? Will things change? It's not like the Dust will go away or the stars will come back just because I tell the truth.

And what if I keep quiet? I could bring Denver home after the next mission. I could keep making money for my family.

Mortimer's eyes bore into mine.

You're afraid of Mortimer Good. My heart tells me this, loud enough to ring inside my bones. Loud enough to be true. I've just heard from Iggy what kind of person Mortimer Good can be. And as soon as I saw him stir up the Dustpuppets, I knew—he is a dangerous man. He has the ability to take everything, everyone I love, away from me. I wonder if this is why people pretend they don't see evil, because to see it—to call it out—could harm someone you love.

"Mallie," Mortimer says, his voice like low thunder. "What will you do today?"

I hear my heartbeat echoing in my ears. All the riders turn to look at me, confused. Iggy looks at me wide-eyed. He knows I know something. I don't know how. But he knows.

My words are shaky when they finally let loose: "I'm bringing you back the most Timor powder today. I'm winning the extra Feathersworth."

He smiles at this. His eyes soften—in delight?—or is it relief?

"Take your mount," Mortimer calls out, victory in his voice. "Be brave, my riders."

It occurs to me then that wearing my UtilitySnap on this run might not be safe, especially if lightning is involved. I toss it to the ground, where people have left packs and jackets. I cuff the sleeve of my coveralls to my elbows on both sides. It feels nice, having nothing on my arm. And nobody else seems to notice or care, which is also nice.

"I'll keep this for you," Iggy says, picking up the UtilitySnap and tucking it underneath her arm. "Never know when you might need it."

Iggy reaches out for my arm in a kind way. Our eyes meet and she's smiling, sadly. "We do what we have to, Mallie-girl," she says. "There's different kinds of brave."

"I don't feel brave," I tell her as I walk away. "Just foolish."

Mortimer grins at me as I ride past him, but I don't smile back. Now I realize his smile looks wolfish, not beautiful.

The Lightning Range is rocky, orange-colored. *Like my old Popsnap*, I think. As we fly toward the mountains, I see veins of lighting flicker all across the black clouds spinning above them. The spin is so gentle that it reminds me of making pinkberry pie with Mama when I was little. *Stir gently, Mallie*, she would say, putting her hand over mine to show me how. To slow me down. I guess I've never been good at being gentle. This doesn't seem like the right time for it, either.

"Steady," I hear boys calling to their horses, all around me. But I don't have to remind Leo. He's already steady and strong. I pat his neck and remind him: "I'm here. We'll be okay."

We sail closer, underneath the stormy canopy. The air is warm and electric. A sudden wind, like a warm breath from the jaws of the mountain, blows in our faces. The sky is an abysmal black now, an endless, swirling horizon of storms.

Boom. The thunder cracks like an ax chop above the clouds. The mountains catch the echo and roll it back and forth like a roar. I feel it in my teeth.

"Should we turn back?" Adam yells as we see some boys retreat.

"NO!" I shout. This ride will make fifteen hundred Feathersworth for me, bringing me close to the four thousand I need for Denver.

I imagine running through the woods, giving the Feathersworth to Mama. So much she can't hold it all in her apron; coins so golden they reflect on her face.

The air goes choppy, so rough that Leo breaks his steady glide and gallops on the wind. Working his legs manically, he neighs and runs even though there's no ground beneath us. I hear the boys below me yell as the wind batters them.

Leo drops ten feet, so fast that I'm not ready. I scream as I rise up off the saddle, and slam down with an "oomph."

Holding the reins again, I lean forward.

"Push through, Leo. Ride on!"

Leo curves hard to the right as a bright bolt of lightning snaps down to my left. Sparks fly from the singed place on the mountain where the bolt hit the ground.

BOOM!

Another bolt to my right, and Leo swerves again. I feel the heat of each bright bolt crashing down.

Air shimmers where they strike. Hair prickles on my arms.

I let Leo lead; he steers me around bolt after bolt of purple lightning.

Then Leo dips down low and I see caverns. A bit of a

break, I think. And I flip my goggles when my eyes catch a sparkle.

The caverns are deep and craggy with sharp rocks jutting down from the ceiling. Dark is so thick around us that even Leo begins to waver. He rams into a rock face, scraping his side.

"Careful, Leo!" I try to calm him. "Slow down! Easy!"

But Leo can't hear me; thunder echoes even louder in here than it did out there.

I tap his flanks gently with my boot heels. "UP!" He obeys—gladly—and shoots back into the storm. I catch a glimpse of Adam to my right. He's too busy trying to push Honor away to bag any powder at all.

"Watch out!" I shout. But Adam doesn't hear me. Honor does.

Everything feels like it's happening in slow motion. Adam's horse flies sideways to avoid a bolt of lightning, and his boots lose their grip completely. He grabs for his horse's neck, but rain is pouring now. The horse is too slick to hold.

Honor sails in close again. Even now, even knowing him the way I do, I think he'll give Adam a hand, help him back on his horse, at least. But that's not what happens. Honor stretches out his long leg. I'm already flying toward them, screaming, but I don't get there in time. Honor stomps Adam's wrist. And Adam lets go.

"Leo!" I scream. "Dive!" Even as we're zooming for Adam, I know we won't make it.

I watch as he grabs his wrist in agony and tumbles through the air. Fear spreads its claws inside my chest and everyone around me seems to fade except that terrible sight: my friend, falling.

I'm shouting commands, racing for the ground faster than we've flown before. I've got to get beneath him. But he's going too fast! Adam grapples for air. His eyes are locked on me and Leo. I shout as Adam disappears through a drift of low clouds. I can't see what's beneath it, but I don't care. We fly blind into the cloud as I scream, over and over, "Down, Leo! Down!"

We swoop up underneath Adam, and he lands on the saddle behind me.

Adam's arms lock around my waist.

I feel him rest his forehead against my shoulder, but he doesn't say anything. I don't know if I could find words either after a fall like that. As we float back up in the sky, Jeff flies through the low clouds, near enough to nuzzle Adam's face.

"Thank you, Mallie," Adam whispers. With a shaky

hand he reaches past me to pat Leo's neck. "Thanks, buddy."

"Go home, Leo," I say as the storm beats down around us. Adam's horse glides along beside us. Connor, Nico, Greer—they're all flying beside me. Our bags are full.

"I got lots of Timor powder," Adam says. "That's what Honor wanted."

"He was going to kill you to get it," I shout. "And he doesn't even need it! What's he going to do with five hundred extra Feathersworth?"

"It was weird up there," Adam says. "Honor was fired up anyway. We all get that way when we ride. But then a Dustcloud flew low, swarmed right in his face. That's when he kicked me off. If you hadn't been there—"

"I don't want to think about that."

I see a clump of the yellow powder in Leo's mane and reach to brush it off. But instead my hand hovers above it for a bit. I pinch the Timor between my fingers and look at the color again.

Yellow rust.

Yellow as the morning Dust.

Like the eyes of the monsters,

Like the grit in my boots,

Like the river that cuts through the heart of these hills.

Strangely, I'm not thinking about what we'll earn.

I'm thinking about Timor powder.

I'm thinking about the stories Mama and Papa told us when we were young. About the mountains far away from here. About a river that runs through those faraway mountains, a river with a dull yellow cast to it. "The Timor River." I can almost hear Denver say it, in his smartest told-you-so voice. "That old river Timor will give you a fright."

"Have you seen them use Timor powder in the mines?" I ask Adam. "Is it the same powder in the river we learned about in school?"

He nods. "We used to shovel it into the big furnace at night. The Guardians say it's energy to keep the mines warm, even in winter. It's thickest near that river, apparently. But there are pockets of it everywhere. The Guardians give us extra break time if we find more in the mine."

I'm imagining that big furnace now, how it sends smoke into the sky every night. How we breathe it in all day, every day. The Guardians told us this powder is medicine. But what if it's not? What if that's the story we've been given . . . so we're living it. Even though it's not true.

This time, rage sets its claws in me without the help of any Dustclouds. I lean forward and race toward the clearing. I have a question for Mortimer Good. I have a decision to make.

I swing off Leo's back as soon as he lands, then pull the Timor powder from Adam. The day is dimming. A few riders have returned already. I hear a few more sets of hooves landing behind us.

"Where are you going?" I hear Adam yell. "Mallie, what are you doing?"

I'm going face-to-face with a monster, I think. *I'm going to scream in its face if I have to.*

"Mallie!" Mortimer says, smiling at me. "I should have known you'd be the one to find—"

"I want to know what this really is," I say, holding the bag up to him. "Timor powder, like the river?"

The smile doesn't leave his face. But his eyes change as he looks at me. "Yes, that powder is found along the banks of the Timor River. It can be used for many things."

"Like making monsters out of the dirt?" I ask, softly. "I've seen this same color all over the mountain. I've seen it in Dustclouds. I see it in the Dust sometimes."

"It is the Dust," Mortimer says, his voice low and fierce. He isn't smiling now. And he's not holding anything back. Now all the riders have landed. I hear them joking with one another. I hear their horses prancing around the clearing. But my shaky breaths feel louder to me.

"You make the Dust," I say softly.

Mortimer nods. And then he has the audacity to grin. I can't believe I ever thought that grin was handsome. Now he only looks cruel.

"I'm going to tell everyone," I say through clenched teeth.

"No you won't." Mortimer says this in such a caring voice. "Because there's no point. People have believed this so long now that they're afraid to even consider anything else. They'll think you're lying. They'll think you're just causing trouble."

"I want to cause trouble," I say, pressing my arm against my side so he won't see it shaking.

"But does your brother want that?" Mortimer says, and smiles down on me kindly. Like he's a doting uncle. He's found the softest spot in my heart, and he knows it. "I can keep sweet Denver Down Below, Mallie. I can keep him there for as long as I want. Right now, he's bragging about his sister the hero. 'Mallie over the Moon,' he calls you. I can change how he sees you. I can keep you apart forever unless . . ."

I gulp, swallowing down a terrible stinging feeling in my throat. I will not let him see me cry. "Unless?"

"Unless you keep all these discoveries a secret." His voice is easy, as if we're having a conversation about the weather. But I can't get past the sharp gleam of his eyes.

Mortimer clears his throat and nods to one of his Guardians. They're going to measure our Keeps. Same as always. Like it's any other day.

"You have a choice," Mortimer says, resting his gloved hand on my shoulder. I stiffen at the feel of it. "Choose carefully, mountain girl."

A Guardian is suddenly at Mortimer's side. "Did she complete the mission? Do you have Dust to weigh?"

"Yes," I say, dropping my eyes to the ground. I hold the bag out to the Guardian.

"Good girl," Mortimer says softly, and he turns to walk away.

The Guardian hands me two bags of Feathersworth. But this time, the money doesn't fill me with hope or pride. I think about Iggy, how we're in the same position, really. We're both doing what we're told, believing Mortimer will give us enough money to take care of the people we love.

But I realize now that he'll just find some other reason to keep Iggy's papa away from her. To keep my brother Down Below. It doesn't matter how many missions I complete, how many Feathersworth I earn.

"Excuse me." Iggy stands beside me, clearing her throat. She holds out my UtilitySnap. "I've been keeping this for you. In case you need it." When I reach to take it, she rests her little hand on top of mine. "I'm with you. I'll help you. Whatever you do."

Mortimer and the Guardians have moved across the clearing, talking to Honor and his friends.

"Keep an eye on things here until you hear from me," I tell Iggy as I fasten the UtiltySnap in place. "I'm going to cause trouble."

Iggy smiles so wide that both cheeks dimple. "I figured."

I stomp toward Adam and the boys from Coal Top. When they see me, they stop talking. I tell Greer, Connor, and Nico to hide my parents. "Granny Mab will help you," I say quietly. "Tell them I'm okay. To trust me. I'll tell you more as soon as I can."

"I'm going with you," Adam says to me. "Wherever you're going."

"Good" I say as I mount my horse. He does the same. "Leo, run. And fly."

"Where are those two headed?" I hear a Guardian shout as we soar skyward.

I look back and see Mortimer watching us. Our eyes meet briefly, long enough for me to see that wolfish grin stretch across his face.

We fly toward the sky so fast my face burns, and then we pivot toward the mountain mines.

21

The Rescue

My first memory of the mines came when I was holding my mama's hand. I remember the way the woods felt: cold and wet. And how they smelled: like peppermint and lavender. We swung a lunch pail between us, and while we walked, she told me stories. Then the whistle blew, and she smiled down at me and told me to go ahead. I could run to meet Papa. When the whistle blew, he was on his way up.

I remember how men spilled out of the mines, shadowy-looking because of the soot they were covered in. Sooty save for the yellow bird on every man's shoulder. Honeysuckle was tiny then, flapping her sunshine wings when she saw me. And Papa would smile and open his arms up wide. His arms might as well have been wings for me, a sheltering place to keep me safe. That is a happy memory of the mines. But I'm not little anymore. And I now know that the Down Below is a miserable place.

Leo glides through the South Woods, landing in thick overgrowth so we can't be seen. Guardians stand alert at the opening of the mine.

I let out a long breath, trying to steady my heart enough to accomplish this part of the plan. Because I don't know what comes after this. I don't even know if *this* is possible.

"I'm a little bit afraid now," I tell Adam. "Are you?"

"I've got Mallie over the Moon with me," he says. "You'll rescue me if I need help."

I shake my head and sigh. I don't have much of a plan for this rescue. Even though I've imagined breaking Denver out of here, actually being here is making my heart race. Everything could go wrong. Thankfully, I don't have enough time to think about all that for very long.

"Ready when you are," I tell Adam. "Please don't get caught."

"Same to you," he says. And then he turns to his gentle, old horse. "All you have to do is fly above me, high enough that they don't see you. Lean down and snatch me before they do, all right? Easy enough?"

Jeff taps his muzzle against Adam's forehead.

"Yeah, yeah," Adam says as he nuzzles against the horse. "Then you can have a snack."

Jeff floats up above us. With a final glance at me—and a final grin—Adam launches into a run through the trees, stomping hard enough to catch the Guardians' attention.

"Over there!" they shout as they run after him.

I lean into Leo for a hug. "I know you'll find me."

Leo neighs, bowing his head to me. The sound is a sad, high pitch that breaks my heart. "I'll be careful," I promise him. "I'm not worried about me. I'm worried about you. Just watch for me. Okay?"

His soft eyes bore into mine. Leo will always find me. He's a true friend.

Pulling away from Leo, I run for the mine, ducking through the dark opening and into the tunnel. Torches line the walls, which makes the descent easy, at first. The light is dim, but at least I can see. My boots slide as the descent gets steeper, so I pitch my body weight slightly back to stay upright.

Just go low, Adam told me. *The sleeping caves are at the lowest level.*

Once the torches run out, I reach for my UtilitySnap. *Time to figure this thing out*, I think to myself. I rotate one of the metal fingers until it becomes a beam of light. It's not a full-on lantern; just a small cluster of glowing pebbles. But it helps me see the step ahead of me, and that's all I need. I keep my hand against the cold, damp wall as I slink down deeper.

I've never been this far down in the mine before. All the darkness—all this quiet—makes my fears grow louder. What if I don't find Denver? Or what if Mortimer is here already? What if he's taken him? It won't take long for him to send his Guardians here.

I pick up speed, light extended in front of me, zooming down into the mines so fast that I'm half sliding, half running. And then a wonderful sound fills my ears: snoring.

Listen for lots of snores, Adam told me. He's right; there's a whole chorus of them way down deep.

I crouch down low enough to crawl through a small tunnel, which leads me out into the Sleeping Cave. It's just as Adam described it, a huge dome of a room where hundreds of tiny cubbies are carved into the walls. Boys are sleeping in each nook, ratty quilts pulled up under their chins. I see pictures stuck to cave walls with gum. Old teddy bears with button eyes dangling from their faces. Denver is small, so I'm banking on him being in a low cubby. And I'm right. At the sight of him, a sad, high sound escapes my chest. Something between a cry and a squeal of delight. Not so different from the sound Leo made for me. I clap my hand over my mouth as I watch Denver sleep. His chest rises and falls. His face is peaceful. He isn't hurt.

I crawl inside the cubby with him and brush his hair back from his face. Kiss his forehead and whisper his name.

He shoots up, gripping his book and his bear.

"Mallie?" He whispers my name like it's a question. And then, again—"Mallie!" Like it's a promise. I hug him tight.

"We have to get out now, and you have to trust me. I'm so sorry about everything. You must be so afraid."

"I wasn't," he says, shaking his head. "I can be brave like you. I told everybody about you, all the people I met. I told them that my sister is a great hero. They knew about you, somehow. In letters from their families. They'd heard rumors that the Starbirds were back. That there was a girl who could ride them like fire in the night. That's you. I'm so proud of you."

He might not be so proud of me once he realizes I'm now a criminal. But for now, this feels really nice. "Do you know how to get to the top of this mine without being seen?"

He grins. "Follow me."

Denver is quick and sly, speeding through tunnels and up ladders and never once dropping the teddy bear or book he brought with him. His baby Dustflight tries to perch on his shoulder but keeps falling off. Denver eventually carries her gently in his hand.

"Almost there," Denver says, pointing ahead to a nearly hidden, grass-covered door. But just as his small fingers touch a cluster of vines to pull them away, warning bells ring all along the tunnels.

"It's locked!" Denver cries, pulling at a rusted latch.

I nudge him out of the way and find the right tool on my UtilitySnap. My arm is shaking with excitement as I flick the lock and push open the door. I had no idea I would be such a natural at criminal endeavors.

We climb out together into the night, onto a hill across from the mine opening. The Guardians aren't standing outside, which causes another not-gentle word to float out of my mouth. I hope they didn't catch Adam. The alarm bells are blaring. The whole mountain will hear.

"I got us out," Denver says. "What's your plan now?"

"There!" The shout of a Guardian, running through the trees. Denver kisses the baby Dustflight and sets her free. "Run!" I say, taking Denver's hand and pulling him alongside me.

"We can't go this way!" Denver shouts. "There's a cliff's edge ahead! A really high one!"

"I know," I say, swooping him up in my arm and slinging him around to my back. "Hold on."

"Mallie, that's a cliff! That's a long fall!"

I smile. "Trust me."

I don't stop running. I glance back once, to see the Guardians running after us. The Guardians with their flowing capes and shining swords. *Crows that go nowhere,* I think to myself.

I jump.

And just like I knew he would, Leo swoops up under me, lifting me into the sky. I pull Denver around so he's in front of me on the horse. I'm never letting him go again.

Denver laughs nervously. "Okay. That was wow."

Adam swoops up beside us on his horse. He's breathless from running through the woods.

"Where do we go now?" Adam asks.

Denver rests back against my chest.

"Somewhere safe," I tell him, looking at Adam. "Somewhere they won't come looking for us. Follow me."

"Mallie!" Denver shouts as Leo climbs higher. "This is too high!"

"It's okay," I remind him. "Hold on tight with your legs. And remember I'm holding on tight to you. I won't let you fall. You're safe with me."

"Swing skyward, Leo!" I say, with a tap of my boot. The horse curves gently over the canopy of treetops, above the mine. Wings flap once, then again. The wind is wild in our hair.

I will never forget this moment, I realize. This moment when my little brother is still small enough for me to hold. The look in his eyes when he sees me, like I'm his hero.

Even sweeter: He looked at me that way before I busted him out of a mine or knew how to fly a horse. I'll make sure he gets to have wild adventures like this in his life; he'll do many more brave things.

He will live a different story than the one he was given.

The Pember Mountains are bleak and snowy, which is probably why they popped to mind for a hideout. At first, this seemed like a great idea. But the air here is a bitter cold that seems to bite its way through you. The light is dim this close to the Dust, and the cold and darkness only magnify how tired we are. Our stomachs growl so loud we hear them echo in the cave where we're huddled together. It's been a few hours since we left the mine. Hunger, not to mention the cold, are making it very hard to think of a good plan.

We're safe here—for a minute, at least. But we can't stay here forever. I feel defeated. Lost, a little.

The horses kneel down close to us, covering us with their wings. Their warmth helps us, but I worry about them. Maybe they can fly through snow, but they're not made to live here. I see crystals forming on Leo's muzzle. "We'll be out of here soon," I promise him. "Just give me a minute to think . . ."

Denver tries to sleep, but he's restless, tossing, turning, scrunching his face with every terrible dream. Adam paces back and forth, the way he does when he's working out a problem in his mind.

I think of my parents, hiding somewhere in the woods.

I think of the Feathersworth I earned, which are surely worthless because I've disobeyed.

Maybe confronting Mortimer with the truth was the worst thing I could have done. Right in this moment, it feels like I made a bad decision.

"How can I convince everyone's he's lying?" I ask Adam. Adam is close beside me, his arm next to my arm. He's there to stay warm but he's there for comfort, too.

"If there was just a way we could prove it," Adam says. "What if you got some of the Timor powder and made a monster? Proved that it's all just some silly magic trick?"

"How will I learn to do that?" I ask. "There's got to be a better way."

Adam chews his lip, working through scenarios in his mind. And I rest my head in my hand, too exhausted to sleep.

I want to scream. So I sing instead, tracing my fingers through Denver's soft hair as I do:

Mountain girl, lift up your eyes,
the stars are shining bright for thee.
Reach out and take the silver cord.
Braid beauty now for all to see.

"Mallie?" Adam is standing at the mouth of the cave, snow falling all around him. He's looking up, toward the sky.

"Yeah?"

Slowly, Adam steps back . . . and a Starpatch floats into the cave.

Soft as a feather.

Cool like the wind.

I reach out my hand, and it lands as gently as a butterfly.

Adam shakes his head. "Where did that come from? All the way up here?"

I walk to the edge of the cave and look up into the sky, the Dust ever present above the snow. I see something there, something rippling, so shiny it's nearly impossible. And I begin to wonder. To question.

I shiver and sing out the words again. And another Starpatch floats down toward me, toward my song.

Well, not *my* song exactly. I'm singing the song of the Star Weavers. The one they sang so long ago.

The song that pulled starlight from the sky. Just like I'm doing now. The Guardians told everyone to stop singing because the Dust was dangerous. And the Dust is dangerous . . . but only when you're in it. When it overwhelms you. What if there's another reason they made us all stop singing?

"I have an idea," I tell Adam, running past him into the cave. My breath is a frosty burst of hope as I mount Leo. "Wait here."

"What are you doing?"

I guide Leo to the edge of the cave, quickly.

"Mallie . . ." Adam reaches for Leo's mane, keeping

him in place. "That look on your face makes me nervous. What are you doing?"

"I need to see. I have to see . . ." I can't keep the smile off my face. "If there's something above the Dust."

Adam's eyes go wide. "You're insane, Mallie. The Dust is poison!"

"Says who?"

Adam bites his tongue. I know what he wants to say. The Guardians.

"There's proof for this, though," Adam says. "When a Dustblob falls over you, sorrow engulfs you. Fly through a Dustcloud and rage fills your heart."

"I know what it's like," I call over my shoulder. "I know the Dust makes us feel numb; that's why the Guardians use it when they make house calls. Sometimes it makes us feel confused and lonely. It's every terrible feeling and no feeling at all. They made it to be that way. Just like they made the monsters. They've tricked all of us. They told us what to do. But who tells a star what to do? What if they've just hidden the stars from us? What if the light wants back in?"

For way too long now, we've believed the stories we've been given.

Adam points to his eyes. "The Dust causes this. Just a little of it. You can't fly around in it!"

"I'm not," I promise him. "I'm going above it."

I tap Leo's sides with my boots. "Fly," I command. And Leo leaps into the air. We're suspended in the cold white air for a moment. Then Leo drops, falling. To build momentum, I think.

I stand in the stirrups, leaning forward. "Up. Let's get through it as fast as we can." *If there is a way through*, I think to myself.

Leo zooms toward the sky. Past the cave where Adam and Denver watch me. Toward the summit of the mountain.

Snow burns my face.

The cold is aching, biting.

Ice chips are sharp against my cheeks.

One last frigid burst of wind and we're above the snow cloud. Higher than I've ever been before. The Dust stretches out as far as I can see, deep brown and billowing. Just a hint of sparkle patched throughout. And a hint of that sinister yellow.

"We just have to get through it," I tell Leo. "It hurts. It's horrible. It will make you feel empty and angry, but I believe there's something above it."

Resolved, Leo flaps his wings, hard. Again. And then he presses his wings against my legs—holding me—and soars toward it.

The Dust looms closer. I hold him tight. Close my eyes. Grind my teeth.

And we burst into the darkness of it.

I feel the heat of it on my skin.

I feel it like a scream rising from the center of my gut, my chest. The rage falls out in a scream of fury, frustration. Terrible scenes play out over my mind:

Monsters, hunting me.

Boys with eye stains, digging through dirt.

Girls scrubbing floors until their knuckles bleed.

Horses, weary from flying.

Iggy hugging herself tightly as the horses fly away.

My papa, his voice fluttering out of his chest.

My mama, worry crushing her soul.

Leo neighs, galloping circles in the Dust. Trying to climb out of it. The darkness is confusing him. And I want to call out to him. I need to . . . but I can't make the words come out of my mouth.

We have to get through it. But another part of my heart tells me—just as loudly—there is no getting through this. This is our normal now; it always will be.

Denver. He'll always be on the run.

Denver . . .

Climbing through the mines. Pushing his way onto the flat ground, like a hero.

Bedtime stories. Adventures and walks to school and

climbing trees. Laughing until our stomachs ache. The Dust didn't take our laughter away.

Mama and Papa. Granny Mab. My friends from the Coal Top school. Iggy.

Adam.

Tears burn against my face. The Dust clouds my vision.

"Climb," I whisper. It's all I can say.

It's all I have to say.

Leo rockets skyward. And just when I think the weight of this Dust is too much, that it's going to suffocate me, that I'm going to tumble back to the earth like a fallen star . . . we burst free from it.

Free into the crisp air of a dark night.

I open my eyes to stars.

22

The Weaver

This cold, starry night isn't just the most beautiful thing I've seen. This kind of silence is one of the most beautiful sounds I've ever heard. It's the sound of a winter-white morning, the space between the words *I love you*. Peace. That's what this sound is. Perfect peace. Leo soars gently above the Dust while I look at the stars.

They were never snuffed out.

They're still here, still shining.

They're all a thousand different colors. Colors we have no names for. And just like they did for the Weavers so many years ago, I feel the stars call out for me, pulling the song from my mouth:

Mountain girl, lift up your eyes,
the stars are shining bright for thee.
Reach out and take the silver cord
Braid beauty now for all to see.

As I sing, the stars begin to stretch. Like they have tails. *Like they're kites,* I think. And my heart feels like a magnet, drawing me farther up, farther toward them. I stretch out my hand—reaching for this light. I long for it, with every corner of my soul, I need these stars.

And as I sing, they reach for me.

Those long strands of silver starlight drip down lower, like candle wax. Suddenly, they're low enough for me to touch.

Breath catches.

Fingers tremble.

Does starlight burn if you hold it in your hand? No. I wrap my fingers around it and realize:

It's as cool as a wish,

as special as a spoken dream.

I let go of the reins and reach for a yellow strand of light. Then a blue one. I twist the strands together until they are as green as the stripe in my hair. The colors meld into something metallic, shimmering. And I can't stop reaching now. I can't stop creating.

Bending the light into shapes, into braids, it's new . . . but it's natural, too. As natural as riding a flying horse. I tug my braided starlight until it pulls loose, humming as I work. And then I fashion a pale white beam of light into wings. Wings with sharp points and patterns that I slip around my shoulders.

And I feel lifted, held up. The ever-present ache in my back doesn't hurt so much. This light braces me. That's what this must have felt like, years ago, when people wrapped starry capes around their shoulders. When they held starry books in their hands. It's like the light draws the very best in you up to the surface. It's hard to look down when you wear stars.

I wrap spools of light around my arms, drape them across Leo's back. I feel him tensing beneath me, antsy to fly.

"Okay," I whisper, not sure of what he'll do. "Go!"

He's running on air, playful as a puppy as starry threads drip down all around us.

I wouldn't have seen this if I'd turned back. I wish the Dust had never been here in the first place. But pushing through it was worth it for this. I am a Star Weaver.

I've been one all along.

"We have to tell them," I say to Leo, looking down at the Dust below me. The yellow is visible up here, woven as subtly as a topstitch throughout the gray. "We have to tell them the light isn't gone. It's here."

Before we return to the cave, I see something: grains in the Dust, like fingerprints. They have a strange sheen to them, a nearly invisible spin. The entire spiral of Dust is spinning, so slowly, toward a central point. And as we fly toward it I know—without looking—what that central point is: the mountain mine.

"We can make this right again," I tell Leo.

I tighten my legs and pull the reins, turning him back toward the cave. It will hurt, I know, to go back through the Dust. Back to Adam and Denver. But I have starlight in my arms now. And I have a plan.

23

Sword Lessons

The next morning, the sun rises somewhere above the Dust, that mix of ink and crushed dandelions we've all become used to. It's the only beautiful we've known for years. We stayed in the mountain cave last night, coming up with a plan. Later in the day, Denver flies with Adam down into the valley to tell the boys in the mines—and the girls going into the city—what is happening. And I fly to the West Woods, to Iggy's stables.

Her eyes go wide when she sees me and Leo. We're flying low through the trees today, careful not to be seen.

"I thought you'd be far away by now," she says. "You can't be here! You've caused a mighty uproar. Mortimer is fuming. So are the Guardians. He's called a town meeting at the Coal Top train platform tonight. He's going to say something awful about you, Mallie. And you know how people are—they'll believe what they're told."

"Come with me," I tell her. "Help me tell the truth."

Iggy bites her lip. "I want to. But Papa, Fred . . ." Her voice trails off into a sad sigh.

"He won't give them back to you. You know he won't, deep down. He'll always find a reason to keep you here working for him. But I can prove he's lying, in a big way. People will see it. I want you to be there, too."

Iggy clenches her hands into fists and nods, once. "Fine. Right. That's the better, braver choice, so I'll do it. But you've got to do one thing for me."

"What?"

Iggy's mouth quirks into a funny half smile. "Help me climb on Leo? I can ride him fine once I'm there, of course."

"I know," I say, sliding off Leo's back. "You've told me." Once I've lifted Iggy into the saddle, I climb up behind her. Leo flies low through the treetops until we're close to the train platform in Coal Top. Dusk is creeping over the mountain. Torches and lanterns are alight along the walkway and against the buildings. We spy Mortimer at the end of the platform with his Guardians, waiting for everyone to arrive.

"He knows you'll confront him," Iggy says. "He's got something up that fancy sleeve of his." I hear a smile in her voice when she adds, "But look how many Guardians he has tonight. He's a little bit afraid of you, Mallie-girl. Or he wouldn't have so many in place."

Her words give me a small boost of confidence, like the small light I had in the cave. I have enough courage to take the next step now.

"Land," I whisper to Leo. We ride quietly to the small, dusty corner where I used to hide after work to catch my breath. I can see Mortimer farther down the platform, waiting for the townspeople to arrive. They should be here any minute.

"What do we do?" Iggy asks.

"Wait until people start coming," I tell her. "Then we'll tell them."

"Is that so?" trills Honor's voice from behind me. "The mountain pirate and her faithful mushroom are here to make an announcement? I can't wait to hear it."

Iggy turns to face him first and takes an immediate step back. I see why.

Because Honor is holding his sword. And it's pointed at me. "Imagine how happy they'll be when I announce that I've caught you. Then I'll be a hero."

I have no time for Honor Tumbrel today. I've never had time for him.

My eyes dart to a lattice hanging overhead, the one where the dusty paper roses are held. The squares are big up there. Big enough to fall down over his shoulders just right. In one slick move, I dart around him, running for the rope holding the lattice overhead. Honor lunges in my way, blocking me.

But I swivel around behind him, jumping for a broom propped up against the side of the building. Gripping it in my hand, I spin toward Honor—just as he raises his sword into the air. His blade slices against my broomstick but doesn't break it. I knew it wouldn't. My green stripe of hair falls down in my face, and I see the shock in his eyes. Honor owns a sword. But he's barely practiced with it.

While his sword is stuck in the handle of the broom, I raise my boot and kick him hard in the chest.

He growls as he falls, but bounces up quickly. The veins are visible in his neck. He twirls the blade in his hand. The dull blue sheen of the metal reminds me of animal eyes in the night.

"Go, Mallie! Knock him out!" Iggy screams. She's bouncing around behind me, punching the air like she's the one fighting. I only watch her for a second, but it's enough to lose my focus.

Without warning Honor spins, and his sword crashes into the broom before I'm ready. Another sliding slash of metal, and this time my flimsy broom warbles. I'm twirling the broomstick, madly trying to keep the sword from striking me. I duck beneath Honor's sword as it arches through the air, twirling around until I'm standing in front of him.

Now he's the one flailing at me, as I move him exactly where I want him, right beneath the lattice. I slash my stick against his sword, crank it, and flip his sword onto the ground. The shock barely has time to register on his face before I throw the broomstick down, grab his sword, and spin it toward the rope holding the lattice in place. The lattice falls down around him exactly the way I imagined. Honor Tumbrel is trapped in the midst of rotten boards and paper flowers.

Suddenly, the ground begins to rumble like upside-down thunder.

Honor shakes his head, dazed. "What's that sound?"

"Whoa," Iggy whispers. She has come to stand beside me. Her tiny hand clutches my wrist as she looks out over the expanse.

"That's an army," I tell Honor. "My army."

24

Rules Worth Breaking

Hundreds of children—boys from the mines, girls from the mountain and valley, too—are walking out of the woods with Adam leading them.

Mortimer and the Guardians stand at the far end of the platform, but I see them moving closer at this noise, confused.

Iggy and I walk out from my resting place. Mortimer increases his stride when he sees me, and we meet in the middle of the platform. There's no stage to make him bigger than me now. He's only taller. But he is still intimidating, still cunning. He reminds me of a beautiful snake, still in the grass until the second it strikes.

"Hear me out." Mortimer holds up his hands. He speaks low, so no one else can hear what he's saying to me. "I like you, Mallie. And you need to see that you are making a mistake. Are you trying to intimidate me with a bunch of *children*? Do you think convincing children they've been lied to will change anything? No one will listen to them. Just like no one listens to you. Everything you've worked for could fall apart today. Or, your life could change. We're similar, me and you. I knew it from the moment I met you. When I was your age, I was curious, too. If some people can manipulate starlight, I wondered, then why can't I manipulate other things?"

"So you made the Dust," I say. "You built a wall of Dust all around us, on every side of us. And no one questioned you. I don't understand why."

"I told you once. It's not so hard to convince people to follow you when they're afraid. Fear is a good thing. People need leaders, Mallie. They need boundaries."

"So you gave them monsters."

"I gave them . . . parameters. Rules worth following. Let me teach you what it feels like to be powerful. You could be my assistant."

"No." This isn't a decision I have to weigh anymore. "I won't follow you. Neither will they when they see the truth." I whistle, and Leo soars down to the ground, a blanket of starlight on his back. The children gathered at the platform gasp at the sight of it. Turning to face them, I see they've stopped a good distance from the Guardians, many of them huddled against one another.

"The stars are still here," I tell them. "They're just above the Dust. The Dust doesn't kill you, not like he says. You push through it, and you get to the light again. We'll fly together. You'll see."

"You shouldn't listen to her," Mortimer says, walking up behind me. "She is an anxious, confused little girl. Ever since her father made a mess of the mines . . . she's not been well."

"She's Mallie over the Moon!" shouts Denver, who's sitting on his own horse. I don't know where it came from, but he looks so comfortable already. "Listen to her."

The children are all whispering, gasping at the sight of Denver's horse. Some of them point to the green stripe in my hair, to Leo's wings.

"If you follow her," Mortimer warns, "you'll lose your jobs. Your livelihoods. Why should you believe one girl?"

"He makes the Dust!" I shout to them. "And the Dust makes you feel sad. Or angry. Or hopeless, sometimes. It clouds the way you see things. It weighs you down. There's a way back to the light. We can get it back!"

Low, so only I can hear his voice, Mortimer whispers: "Come on, Mallie. Let me show you a better way. Weaving stars is old, boring magic. I can teach you how to weave emotion into the very air people breathe."

His eyes are on me. But my eyes are on the coal-smudged faces in front of me. Some are younger. Some are older. I know some of them from school, but I've never met most of them before. We're all different. But I know, just by the look in their eyes, that we have this much in common: We are brave enough to believe better stories than we're given.

"Close your eyes," I tell them. "Remember the stories you heard when you were young. Imagine the better-than-best magic. Imagine the horses. Imagine them coming for you."

And one by one, the horses do.

Starbirds I've never met trot out of the woods. Children smile as if they've walked inside a daydream.

"Believe it!" I shout. "You don't have to say it out loud. But in your heart—say that you know better. You are not who he says you are. You don't have to believe the story you are given!"

"Is that right?" Mortimer asks, his voice low and dark. "You don't believe the stories you're given? Prove how brave you are, Mallie."

Hissss.

Swish.

The happy chatter and gasps suffocate immediately at the sounds coming from the woods behind Mortimer Good. Screams erupt from the crowd. The horses stomp and flap their wings. And Mortimer is beaming. His monsters are here.

25

Dust to Dust

Clouds of Dust burst from the trees behind Mortimer, followed by the creatures' screams. Yellow eyes beam, bright and hungry, from the trees. These eyes are high above the ground. The monsters have never been this big before. Even though I know they're only Dust, I'm backing away from them, too. It's like my body is reacting apart from my mind. I know they're not real but I'm still shaking.

The train platform has turned to chaos. My plan

begins crumbling apart. Mortimer crosses his arms over his chest and watches, like it's all just a show, put on for his entertainment.

I take another step back and bump into Leo. He won't let me run away, and I love him for it. I also know he won't let me fight alone. As the monsters emerge from the trees, I try to calm myself. Just because I feel fear doesn't mean there's anything to be afraid of right now.

Weave emotion into the air, Mortimer said. Can he really do that? Is that part of his magic? Are the monsters growing because we're afraid?

There are so many of them—a pack like wolves— some barely distinguishable from the night and shadows. All surrounded in Dust thick enough to smell from here. They're covered in thick scales. Long-clawed paws attach to muscled legs. And when they roar—that earsplitting scream—their long, sharp fangs drip with Dustblobs.

They're Dust, I remind myself. Dustpuppets.

I feel the distance growing between me and the rest of the mountain kids. They've backed up. Their horses are snarling, stomping. This is chaos. A terrible storm that I can't fly away from.

And then I feel a small presence on my other side. Iggy Thump.

My body shakes so hard it trembles, but she's there, bright-eyed. Ready.

"Hold your ground," she says. "Scream in their faces. Do. Not. Run."

I nod my head, embarrassed by the fearful tears running down my face.

One of the creatures catches my eye, holds me in its gaze, then runs for me.

Screaming.

Eyes shining.

Long claws extended.

He's close, a foot away, and I let loose the loudest scream I can find, the roar that's been building in me for as long as I can remember.

I swing it at the first monster, and the beast explodes into a sparkling pouf of Dust. Adam and his horse fly into the direct center of the next one. They're only Dust, but they're still vicious, their claws are still sharp, and I see Adam flinch as one claw swipes his face before the beast explodes.

"What's happening?" It's the voice of an adult, and it's joined by many more. Greer was in charge of getting the grown-ups here. Unfortunately, they've shown up at the same time as the monsters have.

You would think some of the adults behind us would realize what we're doing and run toward us to help. But they don't.

"Come home with me!" I hear a mother scream to a little girl standing near the front. She's trying to pick her up, trying to run with her. But the girl won't have it. She wriggles away every time.

None of the children leave.

Instead, they charge.

Girls I've known from school, girls who've ended up in the valley like me, come running down the platform, broomsticks lifted high over their heads, screaming. They defeat the monsters with their wild chorus of roars. I realize, for the first time, how many of them are wearing green stripes in their hair like mine.

"Mallie"—Adam points—"look!"

Connor and Nico fly onto the platform, my parents behind them. I make eye contact with them for a split second before a monster's claw swipes at my face. I whirl around and punch it in the snout with my UtilitySnap. Its roar disappears in a pouf of glittery dust.

Some of the adults are fighting monsters now, alongside their children. Others are reaching out for the horses. Petting them. Nuzzling their faces.

"They told me you were gone," I hear an old woman

say as she leans a tired, wrinkled cheek against a horse's side.

They told us so many things, and we believed them . . .

An idea crashes against my heart. I run for my parents.

I press my hand against Papa's chest. "Sing out," I tell him. "Believe you can do it, and try. I don't think you ever lost your voice. I think the Guardians convinced you that you did. But it's still there. I believe it's there."

Mama and I watch him, waiting. He squeezes his eyes shut tight.

At first, he opens his mouth, and there is nothing.

But then his voice comes out as a squeak, then a rumble. Then a song:

Mountain girl, lift up your eyes,
The stars are shining bright for thee . . .

Silence falls all around us for a moment. Mama's hand is pressed over her mouth as she watches.

Mama and I sing with him:

Reach out and take the silver cord,
Braid beauty there for all to see.

As we sing, the sky begins to fall.

26

Stars

Maybe it's because we're here, side by side. Because my voice sounds so strong when it echoes all these other voices. Maybe it's because we are determined. We are decided.

Whatever the reason, our voices don't flutter out of our chests like birds. But they do rise toward the skies. There is a strange and wonderful magic when that happens, when voices combine and unite and press against the Dust.

More monsters are surrounding us, but they're dust; all they can do is howl. Maybe bite. They're cheap magic tricks made from Timor powder. Tricks that came from the mind of a terrible man.

And the more we sing, the more Mortimer Good is the one who begins to look afraid.

Zigzag fault lines of light appear across the Dust. The light is a vein, then a river. A booming crack, and the Dust gives way to glorious, cool moonlight. The Dust is broken. Falling in pieces to the ground.

Mortimer screams and calls for his Guardians. They're frantic, throwing handfuls of yellow Timor powder to the ground, sending new monsters swirling up around us. The beasts growl in our faces.

I see Greer's eyes, teary with fear as a monster rounds on him, baring its teeth. But Greer closes his eyes—pretends to be somewhere else—and sings anyway.

The girls from the valley are teaching the boys from the mines how to fight, how to smash the monsters. We fight them with songs. With our voices. We run *at* the beasts instead of running away. Some of the monsters dissolve and explode.

Others begin to wilt, to fall like puppets.

"The Dust will weigh them down," I hear Mortimer mumble as patches of Dust fall fast and close to us.

But the horses will have none of that; they gallop through the crowd, shielding families from falling Dust with their mighty wings.

People huddle, holding one another. The wild fear in their eyes is turning to something wilder—hope.

Leo neighs and rears up on his hind legs, pawing at the air in excitement. The Dust looks like a puzzle above us, missing pieces all around.

And as we sing, through those gaping holes in the Dust, beams of starlight float down. They're ribbons and rods, reaching for us. We reach for them, too—just like our parents did before us. We wrap starlight around our shoulders like blankets. Like capes. Night is beautiful with the full face of the moon shining down on us. With a sky full of light. With stars on our shoulders.

We are shining now, I think. Brighter than the flames of Truth and Flame Mountain. People will see our light for miles.

"Mallie." Mama is behind me, and her is hair down and wavy. I don't know that I've ever seen her hair down before. She ties it up as soon as she wakes. Now that it's long and loose, I see what's been hidden for so long a bolt of dark green. Just like mine.

"You . . . were a Weaver?" I ask.

Mab scuttles over to where we stand, her face alight

with joy. "She was the best Weaver, Mallie-girl. A true mountain hero!"

Mama shakes her head. "Never a hero. I believed what they told me. I thought the stars were gone. The horses were gone. In my heart, I think I knew. But I kept doing what I was told. If I had trusted my heart . . ."

I loop my arms around her waist and hold her tight. Because regret is like Dust—it only weighs you down, only keeps you from seeing all the good ahead. "We found a way," I tell her.

An image settles in my mind of Mama weaving all the starlight she collected—of piles of it on the cottage floor she wove into a thousand wonderful things. Maybe that's why our cottage has always felt like a bright spot to me. I've always seen galaxies in my mother's eyes.

All around us, monsters crumble. They dissolve into piles of yellow dust.

"Mortimer Good!" someone shouts. "He's gone!"

"We should find him." Adam looks at me. "What if he does this somewhere else?"

"He won't," I say. Because in my dreams, I've seen it: We're going to go past the boundaries of Forgotten Mountain. We're going to see other places, and if Mortimer Good—any of the Guardians—end up there, we'll find them. We'll drive them out again. We'll guard the land from the skies, from the backs of our horses.

And the view here on land isn't so bad, either. I can see every mountain I've climbed from here. Many more I've never even heard of. The world is fine, and bright, and enormous, and it calls to us all. The world is begging us to fly. It compels us to climb.

The horses are leaping, jumping in delight. There are new starbirds now that I haven't seen yet, prancing though the crowd to meet new kids arriving on the platform.

Adam nudges Iggy, who has finally thrown off her old mushroom hat.

A small pony with pink stripes in its mane trots through the crowd to meet her. She doesn't say Fred's name. She doesn't have to. Her arms are around him. Tears trickle down her small face. Fred nuzzles her cheek, so happy to be reunited with his best friend. Iggy's papa comes running toward her next, arms stretched wide as a Starbird in flight.

Adam looks at me. Then at her. "How about we give all these newbies a riding lesson?"

Iggy's hugging Fred gently, dearly. Like she'll never let him go. "Not a bad thought," she says, finally. "View's probably marvelous now, with all that Dust gone."

So we climb on our horses. We ride together into the woods.

Leaping.

Then soaring.

Then curving upward, into the light of the brightest night we've ever seen.

On both sides of me, as far as I can see, are riders and horses, just soaring through the skies. And the stars are here somewhere, too, I think. Even when we can't see them.

We are the kings and queens of this mountain.

We're here to bring back the light.

Epilogue

A final truth:

Years ago, in a place called Forgotten Mountain, people only told sad stories. But stories change as time goes on. People do, too. Now the mountain is called Bright once again, and the people there weave wonder from the sky. They tell better stories now. Their favorite begins like this:

Some girls only wish on stars. But once upon a time, on this very mountain, there lived a girl brave enough to fly among them.

ACKNOWLEDGMENTS

Many individuals have helped shape Mallie's world and story. I'm especially indebted to Mallory Kass, my editor, friend, and the most stylish equestrienne I know. Thank you for endless conversations about flying horses vs. real ones. I also want to thank my friends at Scholastic: Crystal McCoy, David Levithan, Tracy van Straaten, Lizette Serrano, Emily Heddleson, Lori Benton, Rachel Feld, Maya Marlette, Melissa Schirmer, Ellie Berger, Elizabeth Whiting, Alexis Lunsford, Jackie Rubin, Sue Flynn, Nikki Mutch, Josh Berlowitz, and the rest of the Scholastic team. Special thanks to Nina Goffi, for all the creativity and care she's put into designing my books. And thank you, Gilbert Ford, for taking ideas from my stories and making them into such beautiful gateway images.

My agent, Suzie Townsend, is a dream. I'm grateful for her consistent and solid passion for storytelling, and for the way she cheers me on through every endeavor (written and otherwise). I'm grateful to the entire team of creative wizards at New Leaf Literary, especially Pouya Shahbazian, Jeremy Stern, Mia Roman, Veronica Grijalva, and Cassandra Baim.

Debra LaTour, M.Ed., OTR/L, gave this story a brilliant and thorough sensitivity read, and I'm so grateful for her time and insight.

I wish to thank the many educators, librarians, book bloggers, and booksellers who've taken my characters into their hearts and shared them with readers. It's an honor to know any of my stories have a space in your bookshelves.

I want to thank my friends and family: especially the Lloyds, the Asburys, the Longs, the Owensbys, and the Manleys. Erin, Andy, Hannah, Connor, Nick, Caroline, and Mia—thank you for reminding me to engage the world with kindness and add more fun to my life. I adore you all, and I'm smitten with your parents. I'm especially grateful to (and for) Justin. He's like Hogwarts and Narnia rolled into a person, and I love him more than words. My sweet dogs, Biscuit and Samson, cuddled close beside me through many long writing days. They deserve all the treats.

Thank you, God, for the gift of Your Son, for the thrill of hope, and for love that's unconditional.

And thank you, reader, for inviting Mallie into your imagination. I'm endlessly inspired by readers I get to meet, especially young readers. You're bringing back the light every day, and I'm in awe. Steady on. Keep punching holes in the Dust. There's starlight up there waiting.

AFTER WORDS™

NATALIE LLOYD'S

Over the Moon

CONTENTS

About the Author

Natalie Lloyd lives in Chattanooga, Tennessee. When she's not writing, she loves adventuring with her husband, Justin, and their dogs, Biscuit and Samson. Her novels for young readers include *A Snicker of Magic*, *The Key to Extraordinary*, and *The Problim Children*.

Q&A with Natalie Lloyd

Q: *What inspired you to write this book?*

A: I was in Kentucky doing an author visit when a reader asked me if I would consider adding a horse to a book. I thought that sounded like a great idea. I think horses are gorgeous, fascinating animals. When I was a kid, my uncle had two horses, and I loved watching them run, listening to their thundering footsteps, and petting their soft snouts. Plus it's just fun writing animals into stories in general. So I knew I would write a horse book eventually. I just didn't know when . . .

It was several months later that I visited a cabin in the mountains with my family. I remember sitting on the porch watching fog fill up the woods early one morning. The fog was so thick you could barely even see the trees. I imagined what could possibly hide in that fog—what magical, wonderful thing or creature could be stalking around in there? That's when I pictured Mallie for the first time, walking around with her hand outstretched. Something is chasing her. But there's something wonderful ahead of her, too. When I pictured her finding Leo, seeing him there in the woods for the first time, my heart fluttered like a Starbird's wings. *That* was my horse story. I couldn't wait to write it!

Q: *How long does it take you to write a novel? What's your writing process like?*

A: Every novel takes a different amount of time. I start with notes full of images I know I want to write. For example, in *Over the Moon*, I was excited about writing Mallie meeting Leo,

Mallie flying through the storm and the stars, Mallie standing up to Mortimer Good, and Mallie's scenes with Adam. Then I put together kind of a loose story-map that helps me decide how to get from one scene to the next, and I write my first draft. My first drafts are usually very different from the final book. First drafts are where I get to play with words and worlds and characters. Sometimes I imagine the main character telling me the story. Once that's finished, I start to revise that story to make it better. After that, I send it to my editor who helps me revise the story and make it even better *again*. We do that several times. (Young readers often tell me they get frustrated with revision. Authors do too! It can be tough to really find the story you're trying to tell, but all the hard work is worth it.) Usually, the process takes at least a year, sometimes longer.

Q: *Can you speak a little about Mallie's disability and the role it plays in the story?*

A: When I pictured Mallie, I pictured her right arm ending at her elbow. She never calls this a disability in the book (and might not even see it that way); it's just her normal and she's used to adapting or working through a situation even when her environment makes it a challenge. That kind of adjustment is something I could relate to; I was born with a disability that causes weak bones (and several other issues too). Sometimes, when I'm recovering from a broken bone, I use a wheelchair. Even when I'm not in a wheelchair, my disability sometimes means I move through the world in a different way. I liked writing about an athlete, like Mallie, who was finding her own way, too. Also, I think it's important to see all kinds of bodies in books since that's the way the world looks.

Q: *Where do your book ideas come from?*
A: Everywhere! You—whoever you are, reading this—have a zillion ideas swirling around in your heart right now. I think one way to find them is to think about what inspires you. There's probably a song you love that you can't stop thinking about (or singing while you unload the dishwasher). There's a book or movie you experienced you keep talking about. Maybe you just went on a hike and couldn't wait to share your pictures, or you watched your local ballet and it made your heart spin. Think about all the places and people who inspire you and then have fun asking, "What if?" For *Over the Moon*, my favorite what ifs were: what if there's something magical in those woods? What if a brave girl finds that something? And she flies on its back? *What if she had to race a flying horse?* What if her world is covered in darkness? What if that darkness isn't really what it seems? Grab a notebook and spend some time in your imagination; you'll be amazed at the ideas already waiting for you there.

Q: *Animals of all sorts play a big role in* Over the Moon. *What's fun about writing about other creatures, real and imaginary?*
A: I adore animals. I like to read about them and watch them interact. My dog, Huckleberry, usually sticks right beside me when I'm writing stories, and I often think about how sweet it is that so much love can come from such a little creature. I think animals are fun for me to write about, whether they're real or imaginary, because they have such fun, distinct person-

alities without ever saying a word. (Unless you want them to say words in your story, which would also be fun!).

Q: *Who are some of your favorite authors?*
A: Two of my forever favorite authors are C.S. Lewis, who wrote *The Chronicles of Narnia*, and Ann M. Martin, who wrote *The Babysitters Club* series. Both of those worlds made me a reader for life! Some of my other favorites are Kate DiCamillo, Sharon Creech, Rita Williams-Garcia, Louis Sachar, Rebecca Stead, Tracey Baptiste, Dan Gameinhart, Jonathan Auxier, Sara Pennypacker, Kekla Magoon, Nikki Loftin, Kirby Larson, Megan Frazer Blakemore, Lauren Castillo, Aida Salazar, Erin Entrada Kelly, Jeff Zentner, and Jasmine Warga. And so many more!

Q: *What's your advice for aspiring young writers?*
A: Keep reading. Keep writing. And keep your heart wide open to all the wonder in the world. I would also encourage you to keep your heart wide open to all the ways the world is hurting. Young readers have the ability to change the world with their words. They inspire me every day.

Q: *Where's your favorite place to read?*
A: My favorite place to read is still in bed, at night, bundled underneath the covers with my dog beside me. I love to read beside windows, too, especially with a view of the woods.

Q: *What were you like as a kid?*
A: As a kid, I was very shy, quirky, and creative—which is pretty much how I am now, too. I absolutely loved spending time with

my family and my pets. Going to my grandparents on Saturday morning was something I looked forward to all week. I wasn't popular but I had a few good friends who loved me, whom I loved with all my heart. I loved to read, especially underneath the willow tree in our front yard. And I couldn't wait to get home from school and write my own stories in my notebooks. I am super lucky because I had people in my life who loved me exactly the way I was.

Q: *What's the best thing about writing books for young readers?*
A: I believe young readers are the *best* readers—they're bright, kind, sensitive, and thoughtful. They bring their incredible imaginations to a story, and they're so open to sharing how they connected with a character or passage in a book. I still can't believe I get to write for them, but it's an incredible honor. In some small way, I hope my stories remind them that their story matters, and that they aren't alone in the world. I'm inspired by their kindness and hope. Writing for them is a dream come true.

Discussion Guide

What makes Leo and Mallie's bond so special? Have you ever felt a close connection with a pet or another animal?

Music and singing play an important role in *Over the Moon*. What do they symbolize in story?

How is life different in Coal Top than it is in the valley? What do you think accounts for these differences?

Mallie's right arm ends just below her elbow. How does her disability affect her? What does she wish other people would understand about her disability?

Mallie will do anything to protect her younger brother, Denver. Who's someone you'd go to great lengths to protect?

What makes Mortimer Good so powerful? What makes him dangerous?

Why does the green stripe appear in Mallie's hair? What does this mean for Mallie and for the people of Coal Top?

If you had a flying horse like Leo, what you would name it? Where would you go?

How has Adam and Mallie's friendship changed over time? Have you had any similar experiences?

What does the Dust represent to you? What sort of "dust" do you encounter in your own life?

Writing Exercises

Over the Moon contains a number of magical creatures, like Starbirds and Dustflights. Use your imagination to come up with your own magical creature and describe it below! (You can use a different piece of paper or a notebook, if you prefer.)

Species Name (like Starbird):

Individual Name (like Leo):

Physical description:

Personality (Is your creature playful? Protective? Mysterious?):

Habitat (Does your creature live in the ocean? In the mountains?):

Diet (What does your creature eat?):

Magical powers:

What sort of adventure would you like to go on with your creature?

Draw a picture of your creature here or on a separate piece of paper!

Ready for more magic?
Keep reading for an excerpt from

CHAPTER ONE

It is a known fact that the most extraordinary moments in a person's life come disguised as ordinary days.

It is a known fact for me, at least.

Because that morning started out mostly the same as all mornings before: I woke up to an ache in my chest, the smell of chocolate, and the sound of the ghost making a racket in the kitchen.

Now, I'm not the sort to dwell on doom and sorrow. Life is too short for that. But I should at least try to describe the ache briefly:

It's not the kind that comes from eating tacos too late at night.

It's the kind that comes from being left behind.

I think my heart knows I should be filling it with new memories, new jokes, and wondrous adventures with the one person I loved most of all. But that person is gone now. And so, my heart has a giant hole in it. I call it the Big Empty.

I squeezed my eyes shut and reminded myself of these affirmations:

Tonight you could have your Destiny Dream.
Never doubt your starry aim.

I repeated those words while I tugged my mud boots on over my jeans, and again when I zipped up my favorite hoodie. Early summer had settled into the mountains, but the air was still chilly first thing in the morning. I didn't feel cold, though. I felt energized. Just the prospect of my Destiny Dream rattled my brain to such a degree that I fixed my sideways braid on the wrong side of my head. I'm not superstitious about most things, but I knew the day would go badly if I wore my braid on the wrong side.

Finally, I snatched up my messenger bag and zoomed down the stairs to see what the ghost was up to.

Since there's no sense in scaring a ghost who might whirl around and scare me in turn, I decided to declare myself.

"It's Emma!" I called out as I stepped into the darkness of the Boneyard Cafe.

My family's bakery, the Boneyard Cafe, takes up the whole bottom floor of our house, which is perched on the edge of a famous cemetery, hence the cafe's creeptastical name. Currently, Granny Blue is doing her best to keep the Boneyard running, as business hasn't been too great lately.

"I'm back here," yelled a voice that, unfortunately, belonged to my big brother, Topher, and not one of the dearly departed. I'd never actually seen the ghost in our kitchen; I'd only heard it banging around. But due to my home's location, I figure I'm bound to run into a ghost eventually.

The air was thick with the smell of chocolate as I walked into the kitchen. The Cocoa Cauldron was already bubbling near the far window. It was Topher's week to make Boneyard Brew, our cafe's most famous treat.

My brother was perched on the tip-top of the tall ladder, digging through one of the supply cabinets like a scrawny snack bandit.

"Hungry?" I asked him.

Thomp. Topher bumped his head on the cabinet, and let out a low groan. He got all squinty-eyed, pretending to be mad, as he hunkered down to look at me. But I could see the start of a smile on his face. "Emma Pearl Casey, I thought you might be a ghost."

"I yelled and declared myself!"

"I know." Topher gave me the same dimpled-cheek grin that made most of the girls at Blackbird Hollow Community College go googly-eyed. "I always get skittish when I'm down here before daylight."

"It *is* early for you to be making brew," I agreed. In my nearly twelve years of existence, we'd never opened before ten a.m. on Sundays. "I'm glad you're making extra. I usually have a big tour group in the graveyard on Sunday."

Topher cocked his head and studied my face. "Are you okay? You look . . . troubled."

I gave him a thumbs-up. "All good."

"Huh." He didn't look convinced, but he reached back into the cabinet and dislodged one of the giant silver muffin pans. He twisted out of the way as it clattered to the floor.

"Easy!" I said as I jumped to hand it back to him. "If you make any more noise down here, you'll—"

"What? Wake the dead? You and Blue play music so loud

the dead can't get any sleep around here anyway."

"I was going to say wake my *dog*. But that's a fair point about the loud music."

Topher stretched tall again, and got back to digging. He tossed a sack of Blue's organic flour down on the countertop before he dismounted the rickety ladder. I could tell by the tune he was whistling that Topher was about to go into a serious baking frenzy. He'd already tied his red bandana securely around his head. That was a direct order from Granny Blue. Topher likes to let his hair grow long and shaggy for summer, so Blue makes him pull his hair back when he bakes.

I felt a soft thump-thump-thump against my boot, and looked down to see Bearclaw yawning up at me. I scooped her up into my arms and hugged her against my chest.

"Is Granny Blue still sleeping?" I asked.

"I don't think she sleeps much anymore." Topher stirred the big spoon through the Boneyard Brew. He nodded toward her office. The door was closed, but a glow of yellow light seeped out into the hallway. "Her light was still on when I went to bed. I wouldn't be surprised if she stayed awake all night." Most of Blackbird Hollow was having a tough time making ends meet, and the cafe was no different.

I cuddled Bear close, but stayed in the doorway. Granny's is that Bear can't go in the kitchen. She says some people are particular about dog fur in their biscuits.

Topher opened a tiny jar full of dried lavender. He tap-tap-tapped out a teaspoon's worth into a tiny, sugar-filled pestle. Flour dust already graced his cheekbones, neck, and hands, as if some angel had reached down out of the clouds to trace my brother's features like, "See, now? *This* is what a perfect human looks like." We are not anything alike in that aspect, my brother and me. It would make way more sense if Topher was supposed to have the Destiny Dream.

But he wasn't.

The Destiny Dream would be happening to me. And soon, I hoped.

"Emma?" Topher studied me carefully. "I can see something's wrong. You might as well tell me."

My brother can read people like a story. He knows when a smile's covering sadness and which sparkly-eyed look is a sure sign of a secret. He can hear a broken heart in the sound of someone's voice. He's especially good at reading me. The floors creaked under Topher's sneakers as he came to stand in front of me, like he was putting himself between me and the world, as if whatever was breaking my heart would have to get past him to get to me.

"It's the Big Empty," I whispered, cuddling Bear tight against the infernal ache in my chest. "I woke up thinking that I wanted to talk to Mama. And then I realized I couldn't talk to her and . . ." I shrugged. "It aches, is all. Missing her is a terrible ache."

Topher reached out to hug me, but I spun around headed for the back door.

"I'm fine, Toph. No need to start the day all morbid and sad. Anyway, I'm off to see the long-ago dearly departed."

I made my way through the kitchen door and onto the back porch. The screen door slapped shut behind me, and I stared out over the dreamy-morning world. The dark night had already faded to a pretty, pale blue at the horizon. A cool wind prickled my skin and rustled the branches of the big oak in the center of the field. It was a life sound the wind made, a pretty rasp and then *shhh* . . . which was kind of strange considering all that lay before me. As far as I could see, the headstones and statues of Blackbird Hollow Cemetery peeked up from the mist.

I plucked a white daisy from the grass, stuck it in my braid, and set out to walk among those graves, just the same as always. I only walk in the daylight, though. Everybody in town knows you never set foot in Blackbird Hollow Cemetery at night. Most people are too skitter-brained to go there during the day as well. But I'm not afraid.

Not exactly.

Okay, here's the honest truth: Sometimes I do feel like something is following me around in the graveyard. At times, that feeling comforts me; it's like I'm being watched over. But every now and then, I get a certain chill and feel more like I'm being flat-out watched.

I was right about both things. But I didn't know it yet.